I0687372

WYOMING SUNDOWN

THE MCALLISTER BROTHERS BOOK THREE

CRICKET ROHMAN

Cricket Rohman

This is a work of fiction. Names, characters, places, and incidents are the product of the author's imagination or are used fictitiously. Any resemblance to actual persons, living or dead, business establishments, events, or locales is entirely coincidental.

Cover design & interior formatting by: Sweet 'N Spicy Designs

ISBN: 978-0-9994819-9-8

Ebook ISBN: 978-0-9994819-8-1

NOVELS BY CRICKET ROHMAN

Saving Madeline

Standalone Contemporary Fiction

The McAllister Brothers Series

Romantic Western Adventures

Colorado Takedown

Montana Countdown

Wyoming Sundown

The Creative Hearts Sweet Romance Series

Creative Women Novellas

Phoebe's Photo Fetish

Anna's Animal House

Caitlin's Cow Wash

Tina's Tasty Tours

The Lindsey Lark Series

Fiction with Elements of Romance & Mystery

Wanted: An Honest Man

Letters, Lovers, & Lies

Hit The Road, Jake!

The Fantasy Maker Series

Contemporary Adventures

Forever Island

Winter's Blush

-

ACKNOWLEDGMENTS

I would like to say thank you to:

Jerry, my husband, for his understanding during the times
I often struggled creating this story.

My talented editor, Amir, for his toughness and
encouragement along the way.

Jaycee, my wonderful formatter/cover designer who's
always there when I need her.

Horses — especially the Spanish Barbs I've come to
know. Their beauty and strength is a constant inspiration.

This book is dedicated to

Adventurers, Ranchers

And

Horse and Dog Lovers

FEELING DOWN? SADDLE UP!

C lint had only two choices: ride or die.

Fed up with his life and the cards he'd been dealt, he almost turned around and drove home, his thoughts over-loaded with negativity. *Why bother? Why pretend day after day to be something I'm not?*

The question his physical therapist had asked on that dreaded first day of rehab came to mind. "What's your goal, Clint?"

He scowled and then replied, "I don't give a damn about goals. I just want to ride my horse."

"Okay, then. That's your goal."

If only it were that simple.

"MORNIN' Mr. McAllister. Glad you're here. Someone's been looking for you all week. Let me give you a hand."

The stable manager's words pulled Clint from his ongoing, dreary thoughts. "Not today, Gill. I've got this." His own unexpected words surprised him, and he almost smiled. "Just bring my horse around." Clint, using his strong arms, lowered himself from the van down to his chair. He waited there to greet Millie, the one thing in his life that kept him going. His feelings for this horse went beyond words.

Raking his fingers through his salt-and-pepper hair, heavy on the salt, he remembered the day the horse was born as if it were yesterday. The mare had struggled. Something was wrong, and she needed help with the birth of her baby. Clint heard her squeals. He rushed in and, on his hands and knees, pulled the new foal from its mother's body. That little filly grabbed Clint's attention, his heart, too, like no horse had ever done.

He named her *Milagro* that first day but called her Millie, for short. He equated the bonding, the connection with the new horse, to having a first child. He took on the initial responsibilities of the young horse's training, which typically were handled by the head wrangler at his ranch. *His* ranch, the McAllister Ranch nicknamed the Big Mack. The words were music to his ears, though he no longer resided there.

Instead, he and Alice lived in a condo just outside of Golden, Colorado. A condo, for heaven's sake! He thought he'd always live on the ranch. Amazing how everything can change in a matter of seconds, and he had no one to blame but himself.

The sound of hoofbeats pounding on the hard, packed dirt advanced rapidly toward him, leaving Gill behind in the dust. No need to be led. The horse knew the routine.

"How's my favorite horse today?" The beautiful, sturdy Palomino lowered its head and puffed out a breath, ready for what would follow. Clint reached up, stroked Millie's neck, then offered her a handful of salted peanuts. The horse ate them, shells and all, then wiggled her lips, showing her teeth, which always brought a grin to Clint's face and a few more peanuts to the horse's mouth.

"You're gonna ride today?" Gill asked with a skeptical tone and a furrowed brow.

Not pleased with Gill's question, Clint shook his head. "What do you think? Don't I always ride when I drive out here to visit my horse?"

"Yes, sir, but it's colder than usual today. Nobody else is riding." He rubbed his gloved hands together as if trying to start a fire. His breath resembled fog floating across a snowy meadow.

Clint's poker-faced stare was all the confirmation Gill needed. There was no point arguing with the man.

"If you're sure." Gill shrugged and grabbed the horse's lead rope. "I'll saddle her up and send her right back to you."

Clint rolled closer to his made-to-order van, and with the push of a few buttons, he brought out his custom, all-terrain chair. He hated the damn thing, but if he wanted to keep riding his horse and saddle up with minimal help from anyone else, he needed it. He shifted his body from the rolling chair onto the high-tech chair, ready to flip the switch that would raise the seat up, level with the saddle.

Today, as Millie trotted back toward him, he was determined to position himself on that saddle with no help at all. And that is exactly what he did, though not without a few grunts, groans, and cuss words. Ah. First time's a charm. Next time will be easier. Clint felt an inkling of confidence and pride.

Gill wasn't a chatty guy – Clint liked that about him – but today, out of the blue and before he'd taken too many steps toward the horse barn, he turned and asked, "You seen your boys lately?"

While bending down and using his hands, Clint guided his boots into the stirrups and said, "Saw Troy, my oldest, briefly. Went out to Trace's place a while back. We're not close. Never have been. I doubt my boys are close with each other. They're too busy workin' their ranches."

"That's too bad. I'm sorry to hear that." Gill turned as his young, exuberant grandkids rushed up to him.

"Grandpa, grandpa! Come on." They each tugged at one of his gloved hands. "Wait 'til you see what we did."

Looking up at Clint, he shrugged. "Family comes first, but I'll be here for you when you get back. Have a good ride now." He tipped his hat and followed the two youngsters to the main house where he and his wife resided.

More often than not, riding Millie triggered a spark of self-worth, if only temporary, and pleasant memories of past abilities. High in the saddle was where he belonged, where he felt whole. However, those intense and vital feelings were short-lived today.

Before he reached the trailhead at the edge of the stable, he felt hollow and without purpose, the same way he felt when sitting at home in his condo. If he were honest with himself, he'd have to admit to feelings of loneliness, too, despite having a wife and two grown sons.

No! Hell, no! He caught himself. He'd never admit or give in to such a ridiculous weakness. As the senior McAllister rancher, it was time he took the bull by the horns and claimed that role again. He'd let his reputation slide over the past fifteen years, but not anymore. It was now or never. Will the real Clint McAllister please stand up? The irony of his statement provided the heavy dose of motivation he needed, though he hadn't a clue how to turn such a drastic incentive into reality.

Gill's words haunted him the entire ride. He had said that family comes first. Did Clint put family first? He had moments when he did, though they might have been few and far between. He'd had several huge ranches to run and his wife Alice to keep the family together, so why had Gill's words caused such an uneasy feeling in his gut? At this point, his thoughts turned into a monologue delivered to a non-judgmental, captive audience – his horse, Millie.

"The way I see it, Millie, the ranch, and my family are one and the same, so I'm not such a bad guy after all." Who was he kidding? His horse? Convincing himself that he was a good guy failed miserably, but he gave it another shot. "Alice does her part, and I do mine." Clint sighed. "At least, I used to."

By mid-afternoon, riding had finally ignited pleasant memories of his younger years and allowed him to escape from his current, disabled reality. With the custom seat-belt attached to the saddle, keeping him firmly in place, he threw caution aside.

"I know it's been a while, Millie, but let's see if we

can ride like the old days." When they came to a flat and broader portion of the trail, he gave his horse the verbal cue to canter. The horse, however, slowed to a stop. "So that's how it's going to be? Did you forget my signals? Or are you telling me what I can and can't do like everyone else does?" He gave the cue again. Millie hesitated, stomped her front hooves, then took off like the wind. Clint rode faster and farther than he should have, returning to the stables later than usual, exhausted but exhilarated.

Gill set down the bale of hay he was carrying and met up with Clint just as the horse came to a complete stop. "Alice called to see if you were on your way home. I told her you got off to a late start today, so that she wouldn't worry. Hope that's okay with you. You might want to give her a call. Ease her mind, you know? Women worry."

"I'll do that as soon as I'm off the horse and back in my van."

Gill stepped closer to offer Clint some assistance as he'd done for many years.

"Don't want your help today. Stand back, and don't worry, I've got this."

"Suit yourself, Mr. McAllister." He sighed, kicked some dirt, and looked the other way.

Once Clint was seated in the van, Gill loaded up his

boss's mechanical horse and attended to Millie. With the horse's lead rope in hand, he headed to the barn where he'd remove her saddle, feed her some oats, and put her up for the night.

Clint lowered the van's driver side window, and raising his voice, called after Gill. "Your comment about family first got me to thinking and gave me an idea." The window went up, and the van peeled out, leaving a trail of dust.

CLINT TOOK the long way home. Without a doubt, he was on a mission, and he needed a few extra minutes to mull over his ideas. First, he told himself he wanted nothing more than to bring his family closer together, and he'd begin with his two sons.

Trace, his youngest, ran the Big Mack Ranch in Colorado, and Troy had transformed their property in Montana into the Lonely Horse Ranch. Clint's thoughts swirled fast and furiously. The inception of a brilliant plan, an adventure, a challenge began right then and there. The central premise and a few details were lodged firmly in his brain by the time he reached the front door of the condo where Alice stood waiting for him.

"A long ride today, huh? I'll bet you're worn out,"

Alice said, although, between the two of them, she was the one who was worn out. Years ago, the sparkle in her beautiful, green eyes had been eclipsed by worry.

Clint planned to tell her all about today's wild ride, knowing full well she'd disapprove. But first, he felt an obligation to share with her his initial germ of an idea. That was the right thing to do.

Alice listened, sitting on the couch, facing Clint. "Let me get this straight, dear," she said, her head tilting. "You're going to ask Trace and Troy to ride over one hundred miles through the Wyoming wilderness in the middle of winter? On horseback? Alone?" Her voice was shrill, and every word was louder than the last.

"It won't be the middle of winter. Winter won't officially begin for several weeks."

With an audible sigh, she removed her reading glasses that rested on the tip of her nose and gave him a rarely used, disapproving glare – the one she saved for special occasions such as this.

"Clint, sweetheart, I love the fact that you want to bring the boys together again. That's a wonderful, long-overdue idea, but this challenge you've invented is way over the top, even for you. It's utterly crazy and, without a doubt, dangerous." Alice paused. "Did you start drinking again?"

"Don't go there, Alice. You know better than that."
His dark blue eyes resembled cold, hard steel.

"All right, I won't, but I want you to know that's how
insane your plan sounds to me."

Deep down, Clint had the utmost respect for his wife,
even if he didn't let it show. More often than not, her
judgment and women's intuition were correct. But today,
she refused to understand or acknowledge the importance
of his challenge – a challenge that would end in a McAllister Men's Reunion. This was a big deal, a chance of a
lifetime for his boys. Maybe she needed a little more
information and time to calm down. The specific rules of
the challenge were still a work in progress.

"I think when you see the final version of my plan,
you'll give it two thumbs up. You might even be envious
and wish you'd thought of it yourself. In the meantime, I
respectfully request your patience, and perhaps you could
uncross those arms of yours."

When Alice uncrossed her arms and then firmly
planted her hands on her hips, the discussion came to an
abrupt end. Well, at least for today.

C lint couldn't deny that winter was fast approaching, and he knew that Wyoming in December could be far more treacherous than anything his sons were accustomed to. That, of course, made the challenge even more difficult. It also made it more interesting.

He hadn't tested his sons' strengths, talents, or stamina for years, far too many years. This event would make up for his limited participation in their lives, allow him to re-establish his reputation, and be the top-ranking McAllister man once again.

With Christmas was just around the corner, time was of the essence. Clint picked up the pace and gave himself only two more days to finalize the details of his plan. Trace and Troy needed some time to get ready for their journeys but could do nothing until they heard about and agreed to participate in this adventure. They both had to agree for the challenge to take place.

What if they turn me down? What if they think my idea is crazy and dangerous, just like their mother does?

Clint shook his head, pushing that thought from his mind. He had to focus on the positive. Putting this event together, though not a simple task, added a new sense of excitement to his life and gave him purpose, something he'd been missing for quite a while. He forged ahead, fine-tuning the details. There'd be no turning back now. He would convince the boys one way or another that this was something they must do.

"Can you take a break? Dinner is ready." Alice placed her hands on his shoulders and rubbed them gently. An outsider, not knowing all the tasks she now performed, might describe her as a sweet, stereotypical homemaker because, in many ways, she was. But, for over a decade, she'd stepped up and took on most of the responsibilities formerly carried out by Clint and never complained, not once. She loved Clint with all her heart, wanted to keep him safe, and rarely left his side no matter how infuriating he became.

"Sure, dear. Dinner would be nice." He closed the computer file he'd been working on all afternoon and led the way to their custom kitchen – every aspect of their condo had been customized for Clint's needs and according to Alice's decorating preferences – where a crackling fire in the fireplace and the delicious aroma of beef stew awaited.

"After dinner, I'll need a pot of strong coffee." He'd be burning the midnight oil, adding essential details to his grand challenge. He'd call Troy first, in a day or two, then Trace. He couldn't wait to spring this on them. If he weren't a tough, macho ranchman, he'd have felt giddy at the thought of putting his sons through such a creative test of their cowboy skills.

THE TIME HAD COME to make the first call and take the next step that would transform his magnificent challenge from an idea to reality. Clint's eagerness for this conversation made waiting for his son to answer the phone a difficult task.

Finally, "Hello. Troy speaking."

"Mornin' Son."

"Hi, Dad. I hope you've got some good news for me. The last time we spoke, Ivy and I invited you and Mom to come visit the ranch, remember? Can't wait for you to see the breeding facility and the dude-ranch operation in person. I'd like to know what you think. And of course, the two of us still have quite a story to tell, one that I think you'll enjoy. So, when will you be here?"

"Before Christmas, if all goes well. I decided to make our visit something special, more of a family get together."

"Okay, I'm listening."

Clint detected the all-too-familiar sound of impatience in Troy's tone. He grinned and cleared his throat, knowing that within seconds, when he explained his plan, his son's impatience would be overridden by a little shock and awe. "There is one small catch before this year's festive occasion can take place."

"A catch?" Troy sighed. "Why am I not surprised?"

Clint would not be deterred by Troy's cynical attitude. Surely, his son would change his tune once he heard the grand plan. "I have a challenge for you and Trace." He detected muffled noises in the background: a dog's yipping, laughter, voices.

"Dad, Ivy's here. I'm going to switch the phone to speaker mode."

"No, Troy. Not yet. At this point, the conversation needs to be private. And it could be lengthy. In fact, I suggest you take some notes." Clint tried to stifle his excitement as he waited for a response. Troy's silence, although a concern, was expected. He pictured his son pacing around the office at the Lonely Horse Ranch, uncomfortable with the prospect of participating in an event, not of his own making.

Troy had taken total control of his life and ranch and done well with that. He'd never asked for his dad's help and never seemed to want it. Like father, like son. He'd learned to be a loner and needed no one. *Should I take credit or blame for that?* Clint was in such a good mood, his thought made him laugh.

"Just a second, Dad." Clint overheard the words that passed between his son and his girlfriend, Ivy. "Would you mind taking the crew back to the house? I'll catch up with you as soon as I'm done here."

"Okay, sure." She didn't sound sure at all. "Come on, Billy. Bring Shadow."

Billy? Shadow? Clint scratched his head.

"Okay, shoot. Let's hear about this challenge that must precede a family get-together."

"You and your brother will compete in a race, an adventure, a real cowboy challenge. The winner takes all."

"All of what, Dad?"

"I'll get to that later. Here's the short version of your part. You'll ride a horse of your choosing from an area just east of Buffalo, Wyoming, to a cabin located five miles south of a small town named Powder Mesa. If you get there first, you win."

Troy kept quiet while Clint continued his explanation, which in many instances included the obvious: he'd need to have warm clothing, food for himself and his horse, a portable shelter, and a loaded gun.

"Since you'll be approaching the cabin from the north, I strongly suggest you prepare for some high altitude winter weather and bring along a good GPS. I'd hate for you to get lost and miss all the fun. It's wild territory. There aren't many landmarks out there, man-made or natural, especially in the winter."

"When will this challenge begin? And how long will I be away from my ranch?"

"That depends on how much time you take getting ready and arriving at your specific starting point. You will head out on horseback on December 8th at high noon. Trace will do the same, but he'll begin from a different location."

Troy had not yet agreed to Clint's plan. He hadn't given the slightest indication that he was eager to participate in the adventure. In fact, his reaction was quite the opposite: he bombarded his dad with a lengthy list of questions. Not a problem. Clint had prepared well and had worked out every detail. He shot back his list of answers as well as the rules. Yes, there were rules to this game.

No riding on paved roads, or within view of paved

roads. Occasional dirt roads or trails were permitted. Any stops along the way to make purchases would be cause for disqualification.

"I'll be waiting for you at the final destination, and we'll have a real McAllister Men's Reunion with an incredible reward for the first one to arrive, all before the women roll in."

"Our women? Ivy, Hannah, and Alice will be rolling in? How does that work?"

"I meant they'd be flying in, though that's not a done deal yet. Anyway, I meant for that to be a surprise, a secret – for the women as well as you and Trace. Guess that cat's out of the bag, huh?" Clint cleared his throat to hide the sound of his own laughter, remembering Troy's relationship with cats. "Do me a favor, act surprised if you do see them in Wyoming. Are you in? Ready to take on my challenge?"

"Have you talked to Trace yet?"

"I'll be calling him just as soon as you and I have finished our conversation."

"I'll get back to you in a day or two." Troy hung up.

Clint had expected Troy to resist and show reluctance at first, but he also assumed a commitment would follow, but that was not to be. Maybe Trace would be an easier sell, and perhaps Clint's pitch needed improvement.

THREE

TROY

Troy had barely made it back to his private residence at the Lonely Horse Ranch when his landline rang. He frowned, staring at the phone. It had no caller ID, but he was quite sure it was Clint. *Here it comes*, he thought, *round two of Clint's campaign.*

The man could be persistent when he wanted something. But there was no way that he would talk to his dad again before he'd had a chance to share their previous conversation with Ivy. Letting it ring, he opened a bottle of sparkling water and was about to take a huge, refreshing gulp when Ivy answered the phone.

Troy, assuming that it was his dad calling again to pick up where he'd left off, shook his head and mouthed *not now*. He had some thinking to do before hearing any more about the challenge or deciding whether to participate.

She shrugged and whispered, "It's your brother," as she handed the phone to Troy. "We're going to take Shadow for a romp outside – grab the tennis ball, Billy – we'll be right back." Ivy was not only beautiful, she was also smart and used her intuition wisely. She placed a quick kiss on his cheek, and the threesome headed for the door.

"I take it you got Dad's call. What do you think?"

Without any hesitation, Trace blurted out, "I don't like his idea at all. It's not only crazy, it's also downright dangerous. This isn't like Dad. He's usually a conserva-tive, cautious man."

"You really think so? I never thought he was cautious, but I can't say I knew him well enough to judge his personality." Troy stood and paced back and forth across his office. "The truth is, I never felt like I had a dad. He was the man who gave me orders to follow, and now he's doing that again." Troy surprised himself, his bitter tone so uncharacteristic. *I guess I'm better at being my own man than being my father's son.*

Trace was likely surprised, too, because he took his time responding. "He must be aware of the risks involved on a ride through the Wyoming winter wastelands, right?"

"Maybe, not sure. Why would Dad do this?" asked

Troy, a frustrated sigh escaping from deep within his lungs. "But, the bigger question is, why would we?"

"For some reason, he thinks an unnamed reward will persuade us to participate in, uh, Clint's Folly. I've already got everything I want. No prizes needed here. How about you guys?"

"Yep. Ivy and I are doing just fine. If only it was summer or fall, but winter in Wyoming? And right before Christmas? Dad's timing couldn't be worse." Troy stood still and silent before continuing. "Maybe we could talk him into delaying this event until next summer, or we could just say no and forget the whole thing."

"Yes, we could. That *is* an option."

Troy noticed a change in his brother's tone. Curious, he asked, "What's going through your head?"

Trace was slow to answer. "Well, now that we've been talking and thinking about Dad's plan, a part of me is kind of up for the challenge."

"Yeah, the stupid part." Immediately regretting his words, Troy laughed, hoping to squash any bad feelings they might have triggered. "You ever spend any time in Wyoming?"

"No, never have."

"Me neither. Not even in a truck. If we do this, we're going to freeze our butts off sitting on a saddle on the back of a horse trekking through nowhere... for *days*.

Many cold days and freezing nights." Troy didn't want to be the spoilsport and say no to their dad's wild and crazy idea, but he also didn't want to be the one to suggest they put their lives on the line. And for what? Some nameless carrot dangling in front of their noses complements of their dad?

"Yeah, this is too dangerous," Trace said. "We're smarter than that, right?"

Troy took another gulp of his water. "And the more I think about it, I don't like that Dad is pitting us against each other. That's no way to kick off a reunion."

"I agree, but what if we knew what the prize was and it was something amazing? Would that make a difference?"

The silence lingering across the airwaves was unbearable; each man likely curious about the other's thoughts and the pros and cons of their dad's challenge. "Let's do it!" they both said at once, followed by guarded laughter.

"But not without some plans and rules of our own," Troy added.

FOUR

TRACE

Light snow fell at the Lucky Seven Ranch as Trace and Hannah walked down to the lower pasture where her small herd of cows spent most of its time. She continued to live up to her lady-with-the-pet-cows reputation bestowed upon her by some of the locals and checked on her cows every day, sometimes twice a day.

The cattle dog, Oatie, and the puppy, Little Charlie, tagged along but without their usual enthusiasm. Did the dogs sense something serious loomed in the air around them? Had they picked up the awkward vibes bouncing back and forth between their owners?

"You haven't told me much about this trip your dad wants you and your brother to take. How come?" Hannah asked, breaking the silence.

"We don't really want to take Dad's challenge, but Troy and I agreed to do it because it seemed so important to him. We're still working out the details. I'm riding north, he's riding south, and we're meeting Dad somewhere in the middle of Wyoming relatively soon."

Hannah stopped. The expression on her pretty face said it all. Even without the details, she knew they were taking on a risky proposition. Heck, the brothers knew it too. "I know I encouraged you to fly up to see Troy just over a month ago, but this is different. Please don't go. It doesn't feel right."

She often had more than her share of women's intuition, but he would go anyway. He felt he must. Trace wrapped his arms around her, brushed away the strands of silky blonde hair from her eyes, and kissed her soft pink lips. Not a day passed in which the love he felt for her failed to amaze him. "You'll be fine. The dogs, the horses, and the cows will still be here with you. Harry, my main man at the Big Mack, and even Sheriff Jane will stop by to check on the Lucky Seven and see how you're doing. You've got their numbers. And I'll ask Rosa to come by, too, if you'd like that."

She backed away, her gloved hands set firmly on her hips. "I'm not worried about me. I'm worried about you... and Clark."

"I'm not taking Clark. He's your horse now, and

besides, Lewissa would do her barn-sour thing if he were gone, and believe me, that would make you miserable. They're best buds, you know. We might work on that issue come spring. Since you're already a horse whisperer, you might as well become a horse trainer too."

No words were spoken as they trudged up the hill toward the ranch house, the greenhouse, the small round pen, and horse barn. Hannah stopped and looked up at Trace. "This whole idea? It doesn't sound like Clint to me. I've only spent a brief time with him, but he seemed so sensible, so wise."

"Yeah, well, he has his moments. And don't forget, you'd just gone through a near-death experience and were still a bit shaken when you met him."

They huffed and puffed a bit as their up-hill walk continued. It wasn't until they reached the top and approached the horse barn that Hannah broke this second round of silence.

"If not Clark, who?"

"I'm glad you asked. Your question gave me a good idea. Come on. I think you should help me decide."

Trace led her to the truck, and off they went, dogs and all. He drove twenty miles northwest on the gravel road that led to the main ranch, the Big Mack, where he parked next to one of the ranch's Rangers.

"What now?" Hannah asked.

Trace could not contain his excitement for what was about to happen. "We're going to get into that off-road vehicle. It will tackle the snow-covered terrain of the horse pasture far better than the truck."

Compared to the truck's warmth, the outside temperature was shocking. Once they began to drive across the pasture, the wind chill factor added a dramatic degree of discomfort. It was damn cold. A group of three horses off in the distance noticed their approach and trotted toward them. Six more soon joined the curious herd. Humans often came with food or treats, especially this time of year.

"Here they come. Get ready to pick one," Trace said.

"Me? You're the one who will be on its back for days, likely in bad weather and—"

"Yes, you. Just watch them for a while." He had complete confidence in her ability to communicate with the horses. "Any of these animals could make the trip, but I want you to pick the one that wants to go." Trace loved the way Hannah's green eyes sparkled when he said that.

Trace, Oatie, and Little Charlie remained in the Ranger and watched Hannah walk from horse to horse. She paused beside each one, rubbed its neck and withers, and gazed into its eyes. The nine horses remained quiet and relatively still, just watching her, either waiting for their turn or merely curious about her presence.

But there was also another horse, a tenth one. That one kept its distance and seemed focused on Hannah, almost as if it were studying her. As she headed toward that lone, beautiful, black horse, it stood its ground for a moment, then started taking slow steps toward her. They met halfway.

Hannah spent a few minutes with this horse like she had with the others, but with one minor difference. After going through her routine, she turned and walked about twenty paces away from the horse. Without hesitation, it followed her and stood by her side. After a few quiet, motionless moments, the horse lowered its head, nuzzled her shoulder, and whinnied softly as if whispering.

"You want to go with Trace, don't you?"

Hannah and the horse stood side by side for quite a while. Trace watched in awe fighting the urge to join them. What would happen next?

The horse backed slowly away from Hannah, then turned and trotted further from her. It seemed to have a plan of its own. It turned once more as if making sure she was watching him. The horse reared up several times, then galloped back, skidding to a halt within a few feet of her.

"Impressive. Okay, you're the one. Let's go tell Trace." The horse followed her back to the Ranger and those watching her selection process. "This one! What's his name?"

Trace was glad he hadn't put money on which horse she'd choose. He'd have lost. "Blackjack. He's a Spanish Barb. As you can see, he's incredibly intelligent, though not as social as some of my other horses. He has amazing stamina and gallops like a sprinter. He and I are somewhat alike."

She laughed a little too enthusiastically. "Is that supposed to mean you have all the characteristics you just mentioned?"

"No, not exactly." He thought for a moment. He was intelligent and… no, he wouldn't go there, although what he pictured made him laugh. "We're both extremely fond of you, and we want to amaze you."

After giving each horse a treat, they rode the Ranger back to the warmth of the truck and drove to the Lucky Seven, where a Crockpot full of vegetarian chili would be just about ready to eat.

TRACE SNUGGLED up with Hannah on the couch in front of the woodstove while Oatie and Little Charlie lay curled up on the floor halfway between them and the warmth of the fire. They'd turned on the back porch light so they could watch the delicate snow floating down from the dark sky.

"I like the way that ring looks on your finger." He lifted her hand to his lips and kissed it gently. The ring holding seven diamonds in the shape of a tiny horseshoe sparkled in the flickering, golden light from the fire's flames.

Hannah smiled and held his face in her hands. "I love the way you look, especially when you're looking at me." She kissed him with the sweetness of an angel.

If only that loving feeling could last forever, or at least for a few more hours. Trace's love for Hannah was stronger than anything he'd ever experienced before. He wanted to be close and intimate with her every day for the rest of his life. He'd marry her tonight if he could, but she'd requested a seven-month engagement period. He'd created a monster when he'd told her about the Legend of the Lucky Seven Ranch. He'd even joked about it being a curse. As a result, the number seven came up in conversations and in their lives more often than ever before.

The magical moment faded when she pulled back and rearranged herself into a crossed-leg sitting position. A no-nonsense expression formed on her pretty face. "What do you know about the *cabin* that your father is sending you to?"

Back to reality. What could he say? He knew so little.

"Dad's up to something. That's for sure. I just don't know what. Maybe he's purchased a cabin that would be midway between us in Colorado and Troy in Montana. That might encourage more frequent family gatherings. He seemed pleased when he heard that Troy and I got together last month. Or maybe he's rented a place for a one-time reunion of sorts." He shrugged. He really didn't know.

"Let's take a walk." Trace took her hand in his.

"But it's dark, and it's snowing."

"I know. Better bundle up. It's time for Oatie to show Little Charlie a thing or two about snapping at snowflakes."

P lane ticket? Check. Van rental? Check. Food and supplies purchased, packed, and ready to be shipped to the cabin? Check, check, and check! Clint insisted on arranging all the details though Alice did her best to keep a watchful eye on the transactions whenever his laptop was open. He'd been closing it a lot lately whenever she entered the room and cutting many of his phone calls short too.

"Seems like you've been busy. So, when do we leave?" Alice had a sweet and salty way of speaking at times – one of her many talents.

Clint had spoken only of the challenge he'd set up for Troy and Trace and that he'd need to be at their final destination before they arrived. He'd never said a word about Alice going with him or mentioned the slim possibility of the women meeting up with the men later, except for that one minor slip-up with Troy. He was still mulling over that part of his plan. He could figure out those details later if he decided to move ahead with that idea.

"Alice, dear, I know you're going to hate hearing this, but you're not coming with me. This event is something I need to do alone." He avoided her eyes, knowing they'd look both shocked and sad.

"You can't be serious, Clint," she said, her eyes showing her concern. "I really wish you'd reconsider and let me come along. You need someone to be there with you, and I know how to assist you. No one else does. We've spent most of our lives doing things together, being together. What makes this any different?"

Clint was prepared with a brief answer, knowing she had negative feelings about his trip ever since he'd mentioned it. "None of the women are going, and that's that." He'd come to a sudden and final decision, at least for the moment. "This is a McAllister Men's Reunion. Men, not women. I won't be gone long, so please, dear, don't insist."

"But I know you better than anyone else in the whole world. You don't like to cook and, from your brief description of the area, there won't be any restaurants nearby, let alone any home delivery of pizza or Chinese food. You'll need me. I'm not letting you go hungry."

Then, with her hands on her hips and her eyes staring him down, she tossed back his own words. "And that's that."

Clint shook his head and held up the palm of his hand, signaling her to stop. "I don't want to argue with you. I'm not going to change my mind, so stop insisting."

For most of Clint's life, he'd felt indestructible and capable of achieving anything and controlling everything. The accident that put him in a wheelchair over a decade ago forced a significant cutback in his daily activities.

Finally, after years of lingering depression, he was ready to escape from his do-little comfort zone. This included Alice and all the sweet, womanly things he'd come to depend on. Naturally, she thought that Clint traveling alone was too dangerous and that he was crazy to attempt such a trip, but that was exactly what he needed to do to regain and keep his sanity.

It was time. "I can do this, Alice. I must do this."

He would not give in. Alice would not give up.

"When was the last time you were at this *cabin* you've selected for the foolish game's final destination? Were you ever there?"

"How long have we been married?" Noticing the signs of frustration coming from his wife, namely her crossed arms and occasional sighs, he looked away, not wanting to reveal the smile forming on his face. That would be marital suicide.

"Thirty-eight years, Clint. Thirty. Eight. Years."

"Let me see." He tapped his fingers on the arm of his chair. "I think I spent some time there about forty years ago. Yes, that sounds about right."

She shook her head, her tired, green eyes filled with liquid sadness.

He rolled closer to her and held her hand. "Me and my boys have had some distance between us for quite a while. That's going to change, and this adventure will serve as the catalyst."

"You're not making much sense. You never really were what I'd call a family man, not with your boys anyway. What's come over you? Why now?"

Clint was quick to speak. "I can't believe I'm hearing these words come from your beautiful lips. Have you been reading those women's magazines again?"

That did it. "How dare you, Clint Campbell McAllister." Tension filled the air, and Alice did not back down. "Oh, you enjoyed being the senior McAllister family man. I remember when your father passed away. You showed no emotion, no sadness, not even at the funeral. His death moved you into the top-dog position, right where you wanted to be."

"What's come over *you*, Alice? You haven't called me by my full name in years, and it's not like you to talk to me this way."

"Well, it's about time that I did."

"Haven't I been a good provider? Haven't I given you and our sons enough?"

"You've given us plenty of… things, but I think it's about time I spoke my mind. You've been nagging our boys to settle down and start their families, so now that they're both on that path, why would you send them away from their women on a dangerous journey?"

Clint wished he could pace back and forth the way he used to do when she frustrated him. Rolling just didn't cut it.

"I don't believe for one minute that this challenge you want to put your sons through is for their own good."

"I wish you'd trust me, dear. Before Christmas arrives, we will be one big, happy family. You'll see." That's what he told Alice, hoping to win her approval and alleviate some of her fears. His statement, though not a total lie, omitted the bigger truth. He was determined to show the world that he was still a strong man who could do anything. He'd just do it differently.

"But Clint—"

"Dear, it's only my legs that don't work. I assure you everything else, including my brain, will rise to the occasion." Grinning, he waited for her reaction. He got one, but not the one he wanted.

It was clear that Alice wasn't buying any of it. Not

the trip, not the challenge, not even his all too subtle offer. That left him with no alternative; there was no way he'd dare tell her the whole story right now. An odd look spread across her face, one he'd never seen before – a faraway trance edged with anger.

"You're acting crazy and foolish." Her delivery was too calm, almost eerie. "If you go through with this cockamamie plan, putting your boys in danger for your own entertainment, I won't be here when you get back."

"Do you really have to do this, Troy?" Ivy asked. "As far as I'm concerned, we've already been through more deadly danger than most people experience in a lifetime."

"True, but this seems so important to Dad. I'd like to think he has a damn good reason for setting up this Wyoming winter adventure."

Ivy began to pace, something he'd never seen her do before. "And you're willing to risk your life, put yourself in serious danger, all because your dad has a wild hair up his... his sleeve?" She did not wait for an answer but continued with her plea to change his mind. "I've been to Wyoming a few times. It's a great state, but you could run into high snowy mountains or mile after mile of nothing but flat, frozen, windswept dirt."

"I can't explain it, but I feel obligated to take on Dad's challenge."

"Then I'm going with you."

"Uh, that's not going to happen, Ivy. Besides, I know you, and you'd never leave little Billy or our pup, Shadow. It's too soon for both of us to be away from them."

Defeated, she sank into a chair. "You're right. I'll help you pack."

"That's my girl. I'll be right back. Gonna have a word with Kitchi."

TROY GAVE himself a pep talk as he walked to the ranch's dining room. He knew Kitchi would be there preparing dinner for the few ranch guests who'd stuck around braving Montana's winter weather. He assumed Kitchi would also find fault with his decision to accept Clint's challenge. Even so, he valued anything this man, his right-hand man from day one, might say. His words would be brief, to the point, and wise. They always were. Troy could count on that.

He'd begin with small talk even though Kitchi would see right through that. "Whatever you're cooking smells good. Ivy, Billy, and I might join the guests and have dinner in here tonight."

Kitchi merely nodded. Troy was unsure how to begin explaining the upcoming journey and felt uncomfortable with his own silence.

"Is there something I can do for you, Mr. McAllister?"

It was now or never. "Are you familiar with the northern half of Wyoming?"

"I wandered around there some before I met you, and we began to create this ranch, this business. Why do you ask?"

Troy shared what he knew about the journey he would soon embark upon. "I'll be traveling from Buffalo, Wyoming, down to Powder Mesa."

"So, you are driving to Buffalo?"

Troy nodded.

"The rest is simple. Continue south on the 25. I assume it's still there and—"

"From Buffalo, I'll be traveling on horseback far from any paved roads." Troy reminded himself to breathe as he waited for Kitchi's next comments.

"Why must you make this journey?

Why, indeed? That question is still rolling around in my head. That was the hardest part for Troy to share with Kitchi. "Dad created a challenge, a contest."

"I see. When does this challenge take place?"

"Soon. We're to head out from our starting points on December 8th."

"We? Who is going with you?"

"I'll be alone. My brother, Trace, will be riding north while I'm heading south. We will meet up in the middle, not far from Powder Mesa."

Kitchi looked up from his work and, with his one unpatched eye, stared intently into Troy's eyes, something he rarely did. "I don't know the senior Mr. McAllister, but I know you. I hope your father has an honest motive and a proper reason for asking you to accept such a challenge."

Kitchi's point was well taken. Having no accurate reply, Troy nodded and kept his conclusion to himself. His dad's request was dangerous, and his motive elusive. That much, he knew. Was there more to it? Was his dad testing him to see if he was brave enough to go or if he had the guts to say no?

As expected, Kitchi did not encourage Troy to take on this challenge. However, knowing that there was no changing Troy's mind, he suggested a few modifications to the route to avoid the most difficult terrain. He made no guarantees because it had been many years since he'd traveled the Wyoming wilderness.

"THAT DIDN'T TAKE LONG," Ivy smiled, seeing Troy in their kitchen's doorway. "Kitchi didn't like the idea either, did he?"

"No, he didn't." At the moment, Troy had grown weary of talking and thinking about Clint's challenge. "What smells so delicious?" He smiled, enjoying the brief distraction from his worries. "Are you cooking dinner?"

It was a rhetorical question. Ivy stood in plain sight, watching over three steaming pots on the stove. Still, this was unusual. Cooking wasn't her thing. Troy was the cook, the gourmet chef in this household. He stepped closer, stood behind her, and wrapped his arms around her waist.

"You smell good too." He nuzzled her neck. "Good enough to—"

"I need to concentrate on the recipe," she said, interrupting him, "to be certain all the necessary ingredients make it into these pots."

Billy came running into the kitchen delighted about something. Shadow, the pup, bounded at his side. "Daddy, daddy, look what I made today."

Troy beamed, and his heart filled with joy whenever the small boy called him daddy. For a guy who, recently, was sure he'd never have a serious relationship with a woman, let alone have a child, he'd found himself with both and loved it.

From a legal standpoint, he and Ivy were Billy's foster parents. Already, they loved him like a son, but there were still hoops to jump through and time that needed to pass before the adoption was official. The entire situation often seemed dreamlike, almost as if he were watching a movie or someone else's life rather than his own. But he was happier than he'd ever been.

"It's for you. I made it for you." Excited, he flapped a piece of paper at Troy.

Troy took it and sat at the table studying the picture this young boy had drawn. "Thanks," he said, trying to make sense of the odd drawing while reminding himself that the child was only five years old. "So... I do see my head, and I really like the cowboy hat, but why don't I have a body?"

"It's there. You just can't see it."

Troy nodded, still baffled by the drawing and now by Billy's words. "You're right about that. I can't see it. Tell me more about your drawing."

Now, Billy seemed frustrated. "It's all about your trip."

"Oh, sure." He still didn't get it.

"Mommy said you were going on a trip, and you'd be buried up to your neck in snow."

That got Ivy's attention, and she stopped stirring the pot – the one on the stove – and hurried over to the table to take a look. While she studied the drawing, Troy studied her, not sure he appreciated her premature comment to Billy. They'd not yet had the chance to have a detailed conversation about his upcoming journey. However, they'd each learned a lesson about how children viewed the world and often took things literally.

"Look, mommy is kissing your ear with her pink lips," Billy beamed.

"I like that part. So this is a happy picture?"

"Oh, yes! Very happy. You're getting a kiss."

Troy whispered in Ivy's ear, "We'll revisit this later."

Ivy went back to the stove and began to dish up their dinner. She insisted it was beef stroganoff.

SEVEN

TROY

After dinner, Billy asked if he could take Shadow for a walk.

"It's kind of dark out there," Troy said. "Do you mind if I come along?"

"No. I don't mind. Mommy can come too."

Ivy looked at Troy and shook her head. "I'm going to clean up the kitchen and get the tub filled with nice warm water. As soon as you get back, young man, in you'll go."

"Can Shadow take a bath too?"

"Yes, someday, but not tonight. Get going. I'll see you both in a few minutes."

Once outside, Troy picked Billy up and held him in his arms. Shadow bounded around playfully sniffing everything in her path.

"The stars are gone. Where did they go?"

"They're up there, Billy, we just can't see them."

"Just like my picture, huh? You couldn't see your whole self 'cause you were covered up by the snow."

Billy had a way with words that made Troy laugh. "You're right about that. The stars are there, but clouds are hiding them." The boy seemed satisfied with that answer though Troy wished it were different. He'd have preferred to see the stars shining brightly from a dark, clear sky.

Shadow, no longer bounding, crouched close to the ground like a cat. Within seconds, she pounced on something. She turned to show Billy her new treasure: a mouse squirming in her mouth. Before he could react, a distant yipping and howling broke the silence. Shadow froze in her tracks, perking up her ears and listening intently. Would she run to her wild relatives out there in the dark? When the sounds coming from the pack grew louder and closer, she dropped her prey and dashed to Troy. The mouse would live another day. So would Shadow. Troy carried both Billy and the pup back to the house.

As promised, Ivy had Billy's bath ready and waiting for him. She asked Troy to supervise and tuck him into bed afterward, then added, "There's something I need to do in the other room." Her brows lifted, and her eyes twinkled.

Troy anticipated mischief. "Yes, ma'am, as long as that *something* includes me."

Sometimes, Ivy was a mystery to him. Tonight was no exception. She flirted, she teased with her words, but her face conveyed a deep sense of melancholy. He felt responsible for her conflicted feelings. That thought bothered him as he helped Billy to bed, kissed him on the forehead, and patted Shadow. The pup and the boy had become inseparable.

He found Ivy already soaking in the spa's hot bubbling water, her mahogany-colored hair tied in a ponytail high on her head with a few tendrils cascading down to her shoulders. A dozen candles flickered, and music from the classical radio station played softly. She stood, no swimsuit tonight, and reached for his hand. "You coming in? The water is just right."

Despite her seductive words and actions, attempting to exhibit a sweet version of strength, he knew she felt sadness and didn't want him to go on this trip. Hell, *he* didn't want to go either; he just thought he had to. Holding her close, kissing her smooth neck, her ticklish ears, and soft lips, he couldn't ignore the elephant in the room much longer.

Tonight, he'd discuss the upcoming event and convince her that it wasn't as dangerous as she thought it would be. He hoped she'd be excited about the challenge he and Trace would soon embark on. Troy took a deep breath of the warm, steamy air rising from the spa and began.

"Agreeing to this journey was a mutual decision between Trace and me, not that we like everything about it, because we don't. Dad's timing could not have been worse. For some unknown reason, he needed this to occur now, which made us worry more about him than about ourselves." Ivy remained silent as he spoke. "He'd never come right out and say anything about this, but we think his health must be declining. That's the only logical reason for demanding that this challenge and reunion take place now."

She turned and wrapped her long, slender legs around his waist. "I hope that's not the case." It was her turn to kiss and caress him, which she did magnificently. He lifted her from the water and placed a bath towel around her while he dried off, then carried her to the king-sized bed.

They kissed and cuddled side-by-side. Sweet and loving was the plan for the rest of the evening – until Ravel's *Bolero,* the sensual classical piece of music, began to play. The radio's timing was perfect. Would Troy's time be perfect too? He wondered if Ivy knew about this one-movement orchestral piece and its reputation?

Whether she knew it or not, the erotic mood of the music changed everything. They became instruments playing a duet and swaying to the conductor's demands, slowly, softly at first, to the gentle flute sounds and the drums light tapping. Before much time had passed, the passion between them grew beyond their control as they kept up with every beat, every note.

The volume grew louder with the addition of the bassoons, and it seemed the tempo increased, too, urging them on. Troy took Ivy's hands, encouraging them to explore, then traced his fingertips across her bottom lip. His light and teasing touch intensified as his tongue seared a path down her slender abdomen, all the way to her thighs, where it lingered but not for long.

Ivy arched her back, rising up to meet him. She was ready, so was he. Time was of the essence. After Troy guided his firm shaft into her soft wetness, it took only seconds before they resumed their roles with the orchestra, only this time as one. Their bodies pounding, surging, heart rates off the charts. His mouth covered hers with a hunger he'd never known before.

Breathless, reeling with ecstasy and in tune with the throbbing, the pulsing of the music, they both knew the end was near when it came to an untimely, sudden stop!

The music coming from the radio was silenced by an ear-piercing buzzing sound followed by the words, *The*

National Weather Service has issued a winter storm warning for southern Montana to central Wyoming. This warning is in effect from 2 AM through 6 PM tomorrow.

Ivy, her wavy hair tousled and damp, her body glistening, sat up and shook her head. From the look on her flushed and worried face, any convincing of the journey's low risk regarding danger would be far more difficult. And now, he had to convince himself too.

EIGHT

ALICE

Alice, unable to persuade her husband to give up his wild idea, decided to focus on the welfare of her sons and their fiancés. While Clint rested, she went into his den, his private space decorated specifically for his mobility needs and resembling his old ranch office. She looked through his address book for Hannah's and Ivy's phone numbers. Not remembering Hannah's last name and never knowing Ivy's, her quest took a while.

She came across a dozen or more names, numbers, and email addresses she didn't recognize during her search. Most of them were female. Her imagination went south, and she recalled all the times when Clint had been on the phone and had suddenly hung up, or when he'd closed his laptop when she'd entered the room. *Don't go there. Do NOT go there.* Surely, he had a reasonable explanation for the presence of the women's names, numbers, and addresses. Sensibly, she moved on to the business at hand.

Donning her warm, furry winter jacket, she headed out the door and down the ramp to conduct a semi-private walk-and-talk. She took a few deep breaths and put on a happy face to help her voice sound optimistic and confident before setting up a conference call with Hannah and Ivy.

"Hi, Hannah. It's Alice. Alice McAllister. Is Trace around?"

"No, I'm sorry. He went into town this morning, but he'll be—"

"Good, because I called to talk to you. Well, you and Ivy. This is a conversation for us McAllister women. Hang on while I try to add Ivy to the call."

"Uh, okay. Sure."

"Ivy? This is Alice, Troy's mother. Is this a good time to talk? I've got Hannah on the line too."

"Absolutely! Hi Hannah," she said, her voice bubbling with excitement. "I'm walking our pup, but I'll make sure I stay within cell service range."

"Can I assume that you both know your men are soon to embark on... what shall we call it?"

Hannah jumped right in. "Mr. Toad's Wild Ride?"

That encouraged Ivy to throw in her two cents. "How about Cowboys Snowboard Mount St. Helens?"

Alice laughed, happy the call got off to a good start. "I see we're all on a similar page. But since we weren't invited to participate in this adventure, I just wanted to make sure you're going to be all right without your men for a couple of weeks. And, please know that we can keep in touch and share any news that we might receive from any of our men."

She gave the gals her landline and cell phone numbers and assured them that the men would be fine. "It's a guy thing, a real cowboy, macho thing. They need this adventure."

Her words did not reflect her true feelings or concerns, but she didn't want them to worry. Behind closed doors, she'd worry enough for all of them. She had three men to think about and pray for. Her boys would face the greatest danger out there in freezing temperatures and miles from civilization.

Clint, though not in any danger Mother Nature might bestow, should not be traveling such a great distance by himself. His metal mustang was heavy, and she wondered how the airport personnel would deal with it. He'd always needed her help just to get it into their van or onto the trailer when they took short trips together – Alice had developed quite a talent for riding that mustang.

Except for riding his horse, Millie, Clint had done little more than watch TV and complain for the past fifteen years. That was what made his plan so shocking to her. Soon, he'd be taking off on an airplane and meeting his sons in the middle of Wyoming all on his own. The more she thought about Clint's plan, the more dangerous it seemed.

I can't let this happen.

She hemmed and hawed about calling her sons. If they said no to Clint, she could stop worrying, even though he'd be disappointed, and his irritability would escalate. She could deal with that, but Trace and Troy might not appreciate her meddling in their business or her opinion about the trip. She convinced herself to stay out of it for now, but memories of that fateful night long ago when she and Clint had argued flooded in.

He'd stormed out and galloped off on his favorite horse, Rowdy. She'd coped with the tragedy by pushing it from her thoughts and focusing only on helping Clint navigate his changed life, but now those memories sent uncomfortable chills up her spine. A magnificent horse died that night, and Clint never walked again.

Trace was certain their goodbye kiss would qualify for entry into the Guinness Book of World Records in several categories: the longest kiss, the hottest kiss, the most heartfelt kiss, but also, maybe, the saddest kiss. Holding Hannah close, he whispered into her ear, "I'll be back in two weeks, darlin', maybe sooner. I'm taking my cell phone so that you can call me any time, day or night."

Hannah didn't want Trace to go, and he, at best, had mixed feelings about Clint's challenge. He wondered if such thoughts had the power to place a jinx on the journey before it had even begun. He recalled the Legend of the Lucky Seven as he hooked up the two-horse, gooseneck trailer to his truck.

Some of the old-timers in Stillwater called it the

Curse of the Lucky Seven. Either way, right off the bat, he faced several sevens: the ranch itself, and today, the day of his departure from it, December 7th. But sevens were good, he remembered. It was a lack of sevens that had disaster potential.

As he drove down the Lucky Seven's long, dirt driveway, he saw them all in his rearview mirror watching him leave: the horses, Lewissa and Clark; Oatie, his all-time favorite dog; and Hannah, the love of his life, holding Little Charlie in her arms. He honked and waved, and the words *I'll be back in two weeks* pounded over and over in his head. The mantra generated no improvement to his state of mind because, ultimately, his private thoughts tagged on the words *if I survive*.

Trace pulled out a day earlier than his brother. He and Blackjack had a two hundred and sixty-six-mile drive to their official starting point, one hundred miles more than Troy had to drive with his horse, Gunner. Due to the additional mileage, an extra day to eat, sleep, and take inventory of the supplies for himself and the horse was agreed upon. Forgetting any items was not an option. If they stuck to Dad's rules, there could be no stopping at stores or homes along the way.

Every mile was uncharted territory as far as Trace was concerned. With Hannah's assistance, he'd planned his journey using a topographical map, knowing it would help, though nature-made detours would likely pop up. The weather reigned at the top of his unseen list of inevitable problems. Uncertainty and his horse were the only things he could count on.

Trace wasn't fond of trailering his horses any further than necessary. Except for the occasional trip to a vet for a procedure in need of technology unavailable at the ranch, his animals spent their days in the pasture or on trails adjacent to it. Wanting to make this new experience for Blackjack as good as he could, he drove into a rest stop along Interstate 25, a location approximately halfway to their official starting point in Bosler, Wyoming. They both rested.

Blackjack, unaccustomed to standing still for so long, was raring to go somewhere, anywhere. Trace was happy to oblige. The horse backed out of the trailer so fast, he almost knocked Trace to the ground. "Whoa, boy. Easy now."

"Hey, cowboy. Is that a wild horse?"

Trace turned and saw who'd asked that question – a woman in skin-tight jeans and a top cut far too low to be worn in this kind of weather. "No, ma'am. He doesn't like to be cooped up or stand still for long. He'll be fine. He just needs some action."

As the woman slinked closer, nibbling her lip, Trace took a step backward and wondered, *What the hell?*

"I need some action too."

It took a minute, but Trace finally got it. Wisely, he mounted up, tipped his hat, and said, "Well, I hope you find some."

For a brief moment, he thought of how lucky he was to have Hannah, an intelligent, sweet, beautiful woman, in his life. Then, he proceeded to ride bareback to an area behind the rest stop consisting of packed, gray dirt and dead, yellow grass. No saddle, no reins, no bit. Trace could direct the horse's movements by shifting the weight of his seat and legs. His dad had taught him how to do that when he was just a boy.

Twenty minutes later, they were on the road again. They continued north to Cheyenne, where they'd hook up with Interstate 80 and head west, then watch for a smaller road that would take them to Bosler. So far, so good. Trace's only complaint? The hole he felt in his heart being so far away from Hannah. He missed her already and would call her once he and his horse settled in later that day.

Trace looked forward to spending some time in Bosler. The town had history. Old Wild West history. Hannah had pointed that out to him in great detail. The famous – and infamous – Tom Horn had quite a career out west, including some time in Bosler. He'd been a scout, a cowboy, a soldier, a range detective, and a

Pinkerton agent. Apparently, Tom had done enough writing about his life that moviemakers created a feature film about his short, action-packed time on earth. He also had a cabin on the Iron Mountain Ranch near Bosler. If there was enough daylight left, Troy would try to find it. Soon he'd be walking the same ground where *the* Tom Horn had walked... before he hung for a murder he likely did not commit.

Seeing the road sign, *Bosler 20 miles,* lifted his spirits. They were almost there. He caught himself singing the old song, *Fly Like an Eagle.* Remembering only a few of the words, he hummed and whistled the tune until they reached the town.

Bosler. Hmm. No motel, no restaurant, not even a rustic, old campground. It was almost a ghost town. *What was Dad thinking?* He remembered seeing a sign for Rock River stating it was another twenty miles north. Twenty miles by truck was nothing. Twenty miles on horseback was a whole different situation, but Bosler wasn't happening. *Rock River, here we come.*

Damn! This town had a few more buildings than the last, even a ranch supply store, but again, no lodging, food, or camping area. No place in sight that offered warmth or comfort. With the sun sinking quickly and with it visibility, Rock River would have to do. Trace drove around until he found a piece of ground on which to set up camp. Unloading his horse, he said, "I guess our 'challenge' begins tonight, right here, Blackjack."

He built a bonfire close to the trailer; then, after stripping down to put on his long johns, he piled on several layers of clothing. Even Blackjack would wear his wool blanket tonight. When he'd finished putting on warmer clothes and taking care of his horse, he set about preparing dinner. He didn't have many options, oats and alfalfa hay for Blackjack, and a can of stew for himself.

The horse seemed perfectly contented, and with a lazy swish of his tail, he began eating his food. Trace shook his head and opened his can of stew, setting it at the fire's edge for a few minutes to heat up. This was as far as he'd want to go in terms of *roughing it.* He ate the whole thing right from the can, deciding not to get anything else dirty except a spoon. After completing this pitiful meal, he took Blackjack for a walk. They circled their makeshift campground at a pace slow enough to warm up but not break a sweat. Dampness would only add to their discomfort and jeopardize their safety.

Darkness had arrived. The fire's orange glow was the only visible illumination, and the stillness so complete, Trace could hear himself breathing. His thoughts waffled between Hannah, Blackjack, and the occasional regret for committing to his dad's nonsensical challenge. He'd debated whether to bring the two-horse trailer or not.

Now, he was glad that he had. Damn glad. He'd be bunking in the trailer with his horse tonight.

"Blackjack, I've made a decision. We're not waiting for Troy to reach his assigned location or our official start time. We're leaving tomorrow as soon as the sun comes up." The horse whinnied from his side of the stall. "And if that's cheating, so be it. I'll forfeit the damn reward. I never wanted it anyway, whatever *it* is."

ON YOUR MARK, GET SET . . .

T race tossed and turned and stood up repeatedly to look out the trailer's small windows. Not only was he cold and uncomfortable, but he also found the space too confining. The first twinges of a panic attack began to build inside him, and his claustrophobic tendency threatened to rear its ugly head.

Why hadn't he thought of that possibility earlier? He knew the answer, though it did him little good, now. Claustrophobic situations were rare, and he avoided them like the plague. Thinking about his phobia was often the furthest thing from his mind until it leaped up and smacked him in the face taking his breath away and rendering him useless.

Recently, he'd been smacked hard when he rescued

Hannah from an old, deserted mineshaft. In addition to the closed, confined space deep beneath the ground's surface, that experience threw both of them into a life and death situation. Tonight, with slow, deep breaths, he was determined to keep his body's reaction to this enclosed space at a minimum. He must.

Here, if he broke into a sweat, he could not go outside to walk it off. It was cold in the trailer, but outside was freezing and would do more harm than good to his body. He thought of Hannah. She was the best distraction ever. Hannah. Dammit! He'd forgotten to call her before turning in and attempting to get some rest. If only he could sleep, he wouldn't feel the twinges of his phobia threatening to make an appearance. Where was his phone? He checked his pockets, then felt around on the floor of the trailer. No luck.

The sky offered little illumination. No moon, no stars. Under normal circumstances, he'd have set the phone in one of his empty boots, but they'd remained on his feet. Trace sat with his back against the trailer's wall and his head in his hands, praying for sleep. It was too late to call anyway. He knew the sudden shock of a ringing phone in the middle of the night would set her heart racing. The sunrise could not come soon enough.

BLACKJACK STOMPED his hooves on the metal floor, and Trace's eyes struggled to open. He must have dozed off for a bit. Though the sun hadn't risen above the horizon, there was enough light to see his phone if it was on his side of the trailer. He looked but found nothing. *Must be in the truck,* he thought, and then stood, reluctantly willing to begin his day.

He unloaded the horse and let it wander free until everything was set out on the ground, ready to be packed up for the ride. He whistled, and the horse came running back, screeching to a dramatic stop in front of him. Trace knew what Blackjack wanted. It was breakfast time; even his own stomach was growling for food. He tossed a flake of hay to the horse and took out a power bar for himself. It took less than a minute to chow it down. While Blackjack remained busy eating his hay, Trace finished packing the essential gear and supplies.

With Blackjack saddled and the saddlebags bulging, all Trace needed to do was grab his phone from the truck and make sure everything he'd leave behind was locked up. That's when he saw the cell phone on the cold, hard ground. At least it hadn't snowed during the night – dampness and cell phones didn't do well together – though, on closer inspection, it wouldn't have mattered. The phone was cracked and crushed, likely stepped on by the horse sometime yesterday, and was now worthless. Dammit. How could he have let that happen?

He mounted up, sighed deeply, and said, "I'm not a quitter, but I could use a little help." He looked toward the heavens for inspiration and was greeted by a flurry of snowflakes floating down from the sky.

The time had come. Today was the day. Troy's starting point for the challenge was near Buffalo, Wyoming. Due to the lack of specificity in the instructions, he selected a location east of the city limits to allow for a less mountainous first day of travel. However, he would need to find a way to the opposite side of Interstate 90 and hoped for an underpass.

He parked his truck and trailer at the far end of the North Forty Truck Stop's lot and unloaded Gunner and all their supplies. Confident he'd complete the journey in four or five days, he wouldn't take much for himself. A backpacker's tent, sub-zero clothing, plenty of matches, water, water purifying tablets, protein bars, beef jerky, and apples should suffice. He would miss his gourmet cooking. Ivy would too. That thought brought a smile to his face, and he imagined that Kitchi would see a lot of Ivy and Billy this week.

Gunner's needs were simple: oats, hay, and a blanket for the nighttime when he was standing still. He'd find water in stock tanks and rivers along the way. Worse case, Troy would melt some ice or snow for him, if necessary.

Troy wasn't worried about this trip because he and Trace had modified Dad's rules for the challenge. If either of them felt threatened by weather or any other danger, they had agreed that it was okay to bend the rules – break them completely – and ride closer to a town or seek help. They were not to place themselves in extreme, life-threatening danger for any reason. They weren't that foolish.

In an hour, it would be high noon and time to hit the non-existent trail. Sixty minutes to lock up, pack up, and saddle up, and then call Ivy. No, he'd make that call right now.

"Hi, babe. How's my favorite girl? It's only been four hours since we said good-bye, and I miss you already."

"I miss you too. We're all fine. Billy, Tracker, Shadow… almost everyone is doing well."

"Almost everyone? I don't like the sound of that. What do you mean?"

"It's probably nothing. Have you spoken with Trace today?"

"No. I was going to call him next."

"Well, Hannah called to see if either of us had heard from him. He'd promised to call her last night before turning in, but his call never came."

"Hmm. Let her know it's probably just a no cell service issue. I'll keep trying to reach Trace. Anything else?"

"Yes. Kitchi has been unusually quiet, and he's waving black sage smudge sticks around every chance he gets."

Troy could picture that. The man was likely a shaman in a previous life, and that carried over into the present. He'd seen signs of that for years. "I'm not surprised. He was dead set against me taking on Dad's challenge."

"He said that?"

"Not in those exact words, but that's what he meant. To be honest, I'm baffled by his choice of the black sage. Where exactly have you seen him smudging?"

"In your office, near Tracker's stall, and, though I haven't seen this happen, I smell the sage all around the perimeter of our house."

"I'm sure he's just trying to be helpful and keep us all on a safe path." Did Kitchi know something that Troy did not know? He usually did. Was he fending off future dangers made visible by a premonition or dream he'd had? Then again, the man had always liked the scent of sage.

"I'll call you whenever I can, but don't worry if you don't hear from me every day. Gunner and I will be fine. Cold, but fine. Love you, babe."

"Love you more."

TROY WAS grateful for the sunny, windless day and to be traveling on flat, open ground for a while. Yesterday, in his attempt to avoid four or more days of snowy mountain travel but still, loosely, follow the rules of the challenge, he'd gone almost twenty extra miles in search of an underpass. Only time would tell if he'd made a wise choice.

He called his brother again. "Trace? Trace! Where are you?" All Troy could hear was static. "If you can hear me, call me back." He assumed static was better than no sound at all and convinced himself that his brother was merely out of cell service range. That was the most logical reason they could not talk to each other and the only reason he'd accept. It was day two of the challenge and much too soon for any real problems to have shown up, though he'd feel a lot better if he could talk to his brother.

"Well, Gunner, I hope you're a good listener because I've got to talk to someone, and you're the only one around."

Troy was a storyteller at heart, always had been. He shook his head and laughed out loud, remembering the time Trace said, "You know, when we were kids, most of your stories were just lies covering up for your bad behavior." He knew that was the truth, but some of those stories were heartfelt and full of mystery and romance. Telling stories, whether fact or fiction, had served him well throughout the years and was a great way to pass the time. Now, his brow furrowed in concentration as he tried to make up a new tale. No stories or lies came to mind today, but a song did.

"On the first day of Christmas, our father gave to us, a challenge needing more time to discuss." He shook his head at his made-up lyrics. Singing wasn't Troy's thing, and his own words held too much truth to enjoy. However, Christmas was his favorite holiday even after discovering the truth about Santa. He hadn't thought about that life-changing moment in years, but suddenly, he remembered it well. Oh, yeah. "Are you ready for a story, Gunner? 'Cause I'm gonna tell you one." The horse walked at a relaxed pace, and Troy began his Christmas story.

Once upon a time, when I was only five years old, I decided that this was the year I'd stay up all night on Christmas Eve because I was determined to see Santa Claus. I had a secret plan, and I'd let nothing stop me.

Rosa, the woman who helped Mom with cooking and housekeeping, gave me a box of cookies to take to the bunkhouse for the wranglers. They were happy to eat fancy cookies; they even gave me one. While eating the cookie, I told them I would stay up all night to get a good look at Santa. The real one, not those fake store ones or the ones in the movies. I was a believer.

Most of the wranglers went along with my plan, wishing me good luck, except for one. He said, "Don't get your hopes up, kid. It's just a fairytale." I didn't understand what his words meant, but I knew he was being mean to me. So I said, "You don't know nothin', Hot-Headed Howard." And I ran out the door. Howard followed me and continued being mean, and now he was also mad. He shouted at me, saying, "Santa Claus is dead!"

I ran back to the main house where I would get to the bottom of Hot-Headed Howard's lies. Everyone was in our huge kitchen. Mom wrapping a few presents, Dad concocting some kind of punch that he said was only for grown-ups, and my little brother Trace toddling around trying to catch my cat.

> *"Hot-Headed Howard said Santa is dead. He's lying, right?" I blurted out.*
>
> *Mom and Dad just looked at each other. Then Dad said, "You called him Hot-Headed Howard?"*
>
> *"Isn't that his name? That's what you call him."*
>
> *"Yeah, well, I may have said that a time or two, but that was a mistake. I think Howard just got mad when he heard you say his name like that."*
>
> *"Oh, good. So he lied about Santa being dead? I want the truth, nothin' but the truth, Dad."*
>
> *Mom and Dad just looked at each other again. They both drank a lot of punch, and they told me that Santa wasn't dead, but he also wasn't alive. He was make-believe. Devastated, I ran to my room and cried for hours.*

"At least that's how I remember it now. No five-year-old should hear that Santa does not exist." Gunner did a little hop to the side, and Troy took that as a sign of agreement. The next hour or so passed slowly, so Troy broke into song again to fill the silence and pass the time.

"On the second day of Christmas, my father gave to us, two tiny kittens, and a challenge needing more time to discuss." *Ah, those were the days. The days before I'd killed my favorite cat.* The next time he broke into song, he'd sing the original version if there were a next time. He wondered what other distant memories might pop up during this long, lonely ride.

He hadn't seen a car, truck, or human ever since heading due south near the Bozeman Trail. Of course, that was the way the journey was supposed to be. So far, except for the trek somewhat near the highway as he scouted for an underpass, he'd violated none of the prescribed rules of the game. If the rough calculations he and Ivy made were somewhat accurate, he would follow the Bozeman Trail for about forty miles before he'd have to branch out to lesser-known trails. By skirting the mountains, he anticipated these first few days would be the easiest of the entire trip.

The trail wasn't always marked, though, and as the elevation rose, so did the snow's depth. Other than traveling in a southbound direction, there were times his location was a complete mystery. So, when the terrain became more mountainous, he made a right turn and headed west for a while. "Gunner, we should run into a road soon, albeit a dirt one that has never seen a snowplow. Even so, it should be visible due to its width, and that should ease the remainder of today's travels."

Troy kept his eyes on the sky and scanned the terrain through binoculars more often than before. The farther he rode from civilization, the more he needed to know what lay ahead – bad weather, a wild animal encounter, or anything unexpected. This was no time for surprises.

TWELVE

CLINT

After a delicious, candlelight dinner of rib-eye steak – he'd been a beef eater from early childhood – twice baked potatoes and broiled mixed veggies, Clint and Alice watched old family videos until bedtime. "Our boys got along so well when they were young," Alice said, gazing at the screen, her voice trembling with an empty sadness. "When did that change? What happened that turned them against each other?"

"I don't remember, dear. I think we just chalked it up to sibling rivalry. Boys will be boys, you know? And we weren't the best parents in the world."

Her sad eyes now glared with fury. He'd said something wrong, made a mistake again. Tonight was not the night to make his wonderful wife angry, but that was precisely what he'd done.

"Speak for yourself. I was a very good mother. You were the one who drank too much."

Here we go again, he thought, clenching his jaw.

"And when you drank, you were too tough on them. Troy and Trace had to compete with each other to try to please you."

"You spoiled them, coddled them," he said through tight lips. "I had to be the one to turn them into strong men. And I did that quite well."

The silence that followed was unbearable, almost worse than their cutting words. Clint had to find a way to turn the evening's quarrel into a tender, kiss and make up affair. "You're right. But do you remember that after my accident up at the Lake Cabin in Colorado, I never drank alcohol again?"

"Yes, and you know I'm thankful for that, but Clint, what is going on now? You're pitting your boys against each other again. Why? They'd just begun to interact in a positive way up at Troy's ranch. You said that yourself."

"The challenge is just for fun. Some adult, cowboy fun. Wyoming's nickname is the Cowboy State, you know."

"Fun? Many days riding on horseback through the Wyoming wilderness in winter is no one's idea of fun. I'd bet money on that." She went back into the kitchen, then returned with cake. Chocolate cake. A peace offering, perhaps.

"You spoil me too." He leaned his upper body closer to his wife and kissed her right on the lips. "Mmm. You taste good, Mrs. McAllister."

She pushed him away. "Oh, Clint, you're just trying to get on my good side."

"All your sides are good, ma'am." Tonight, her anger was no match for Clint's charm, but under normal circumstances, he'd be dead in the water. However, it was rare for him to lather on the pleasantries, so she surrendered immediately and laughed heartily. He guided her onto his lap and gave her a ride to the bedroom.

MORNING ARRIVED TOO QUICKLY, but sleeping in was not an option. For Clint, setting his plan in motion was the top priority. "Up and at 'em," were the first words from his mouth. He moved through his morning procedures with commendable efficiency. "Got a plane to catch, and I'll need extra time to maneuver through the airport's lines and checkpoints." That's what he told Alice as he gulped a cup of coffee and devoured one of her delicious oat bran and honey muffins before beginning his good-bye.

"Let me drive you to the airport. It's the least I can do, and then you won't need to leave your van parked there."

"Thank you, dear, but I got this. I can do it all." Looking up into her eyes, he said, "Here, my dear," and handed her a fancy envelope embossed in gold with the words, DO NOT OPEN UNTIL DECEMBER 24TH. "I'm serious, Alice, dead serious. Do *not* open it."

"There must be something extraordinary in this envelope, but you'll be back by then, right?"

Not wanting to lie to his wife or spoil any future surprises, he merely shrugged and wiggled his eyebrows up and down. He rolled toward the front door, and Alice followed, the envelope still in her hand.

"Just so you know, it was never my intention to pit the boys against each other. I needed to do something – something important and unusual. This whole event, this reunion, is more for me than for them. I hope, someday, you'll understand." Proud of concealing the real motive behind his plans, he added, "You *will* be here when I get back, right?"

She looked away from his gaze. "Still thinking about it."

"You're not going to want to miss Christmas this year, Mrs. McAllister. Keep that in mind."

Alice sighed. "Oh, Clint, I've never been good with good-byes. You know that." She touched Clint's cheek with her fingertips and kissed him before turning away. It was no surprise that she couldn't bring herself to watch him roll toward his custom van using his around-the-house, regular wheelchair. But when he spoke his parting words, "See you soon, my love, sooner than you think," she turned, and he detected a hint of a smile.

THIRTEEN

ALICE

Alice filled the emptiness in her heart and their home by dusting and waxing the furniture, one of the household tasks she enjoyed. Wanda, their weekly housekeeper, kept the bathrooms and floors spotless. She also tackled the oven, the refrigerator, and the windows on an *as-needed* basis. If a situation arose requiring Alice to be out of the house for a good portion of the day, Wanda stayed and kept Clint company. The woman was an angel.

Until today, Alice had rarely left him alone since the accident. Was she overprotective? A helicopter wife, if there was such a thing? Perhaps, but she reminded herself that she was not the one leaving. He was. Still, his comfort and safety remained at the forefront of her thoughts and actions, even when he did not appreciate her attention. Some days, he acted as if his accident was her fault.

He'd soon be on a plane flying far from home all by himself. If only she could have gone with him. She regretted not fighting harder for what she knew was right. A gut feeling nagged at her ever since Clint had mentioned his plan for a men-only Wyoming challenge and reunion. That same feeling gave Alice an idea for the women who were left behind. Another conference call with Hannah and Ivy was in order.

After connecting all the phones – she had that procedure perfected now and could do it quickly – and sharing pleasant greetings, Alice set the stage for the announcement of her brilliant idea. "Hannah, if I'm not mistaken, you and Trace are engaged, right?"

"Yes, Trace proposed at the Lucky Seven Ranch almost two months ago. I can't wait to show you the beautiful ring he had designed for me."

"And I'm anxious to see it. Ivy, you and Troy are engaged too, yes?"

"That's right." Her voice carried a joyful tone.

"Troy asked us to come for a visit as soon as possible, and he said Clint and I were about to be grandparents. Please excuse my forwardness and know that I'll be delighted with any answer you give. Although I can't help but wonder if his statement meant you're pregnant."

Silence.

Then, a heavy sigh.

"I was sitting next to Troy when he said that. And he also said there was a long story that needed to be told by two storytellers. I don't mean to be rude, but I'd like to wait for Troy so that we can tell our story together."

"Say no more. I'll look forward to that day."

Alice asked the gals how they were getting along. Their replies seemed guarded and contained nothing more than a few variations of *everything's fine* and *we're good*. Were they each displaying a false sense of contentment with the current situation as she was? Or were they okay knowing their men were on a dangerous journey? She didn't know them well enough to answer her own question.

Alice had met Hannah when she and Clint visited them at the Big Mack, but that was an odd and difficult time for everyone. She and Ivy were total strangers. Time would change all of that, one way or another.

"Ladies, the main reason for my call is to let you in on a little secret. Mind you, Clint never came right out and said this, but I read between the lines. I think he plans to bring us all to the cabin at the No-Name-Ranch in Wyoming before he and the boys return home. Clint instructed them to arrive no later than December 18th, and preferably sooner. So let's beat Clint at his own game and arrive earlier than that."

The gals didn't answer. There was only silence, followed by heavy sighs.

Ivy spoke up first. "What if our presence is not part of his plan and not appreciated?"

Before Alice could answer, Hannah added, "That could be complicated and problematic, especially if we were to show up unannounced."

"You gals have a point, but I think it will be a glorious surprise. A very special Christmas surprise. Let me give it some additional thought, and I'll call you back." Without a doubt, she had more convincing to do. That would be *her* challenge.

Coordinating a trip for all three of them would be a good distraction from fretting over Clint's safety and his stubbornness, and… she could go on and on but chose to have only positive thoughts for now. After all, he would arrive at the cabin before nightfall. If only that cabin wasn't in such a remote area, and he wasn't there alone, she'd feel a whole lot better.

"LADIES, I've got the beginning of a mighty fine plan. I do know where our men are going though I've never actually been there. To be honest, I disapprove of Clint's big idea – that's nothing new – but that stubborn, macho man does what he wants. After his accident, I thought he might tone down his I-can-do-anything mindset. He did for quite a while, even took that to the extreme point of doing nothing, but lately, it seems to have had the opposite effect."

Alice spoke without pausing as if she were on a mission – a mission impossible – and was determined to make a go of it. Ivy and Hannah listened as she shared what little she knew based on the few facts she'd pried from her husband before he left.

"Other than a property manager from Casper who drives by the deserted old cabin once a month, no one has been there in decades, not even Clint. I'll bet the dust bunnies have become dirt monsters or worse. I just pray that the electricity and plumbing work and not too many creatures are calling it home."

"Alice, it sounds like we don't know what we're getting ourselves into," said Ivy.

"What if nothing is there? Nothing! Then what?" Hannah asked. "Since no McAllister has been there in decades, that property manager might be driving by a parcel of empty land saying all's well, then collecting a paycheck."

Alice chose to ignore that horrific possibility. "Well,

ladies, that's where we come in. The condition of the cabin is the scenario that drives us forward. I don't know about the two of you, but that's enough motivation for me. I want to see that Clint is comfortable and safe, and I bet you'd like your men to arrive at a clean cabin, a warm fire, and some home cooking. Besides, based on the amount of time that Clint spent talking on the phone and using the Internet, I'm confident the cabin, though rustic and old, will be operational."

The gals were too quiet. She'd overwhelmed them. They were not yet wives and didn't feel the responsibilities associated with that kind of partnership. Undaunted by their hesitation, Alice continued, explaining that she would purchase airline tickets and that they'd fly to the Natrona County International Airport in Casper, the same airport Clint flew to.

"We'll meet there, I'll rent a car, and we'll drive to the cabin together. If this odd Christmas adventure is to be to our liking, and we want to spend Christmas with our men, we'd better start packing."

T he drive from Golden, Colorado up to a small town about thirty miles east of Casper had been pleasant, uneventful, just as Clint had planned and hoped for. He'd spent very little time in the Cowboy State of Wyoming, and that was almost forty years ago. So he sat back and relaxed like a tourist enjoying the vast open ranges and the distant snow-covered hills and mountains.

Somewhere between feeling like a tourist and a Wild West cowboy, contradictory emotions betrayed him. On the one hand, he was pleased and proud of his initial plan to bring his boys together by participating in a wild winter journey. On the other, serious second-thoughts sent chills through his upper body as he contemplated the rest of his plan, the part no one else was privy to.

Gill, the head wrangler at Golden Creek Stables, unloaded the horse and the saddlebags filled with provisions. Clint sat in his lightweight, folding wheelchair, watching and directing the set up for his own challenge, a journey he knew would be difficult.

"How's everything look, Mr. McAllister? Is this what you had in mind?" Gill scratched his head. Worry was written all over his face. But then, he smiled. "You're one hell of a man."

Clint paid Gill half the money they'd agreed on and reminded him he'd receive the other half if, and only if, he kept his promise of silence. He was to tell no one about the covert operation that was about to begin.

Already on his horse and buckled in using the custom-made seatbelt attached to the saddle, it was time to begin his journey. Everything he needed had been removed from Gill's truck and gooseneck horse trailer and was loaded onto the smaller trailer that Millie would pull. "I'll give you a call when this is over. Take care now."

He expected Gill to drive off, but the man had a few more words to say. "You sure you don't want me to wait around for a while? I could do that."

"Nice of you to ask, but I've got this. You go on."

"I don't know, Mr. McAllister, the more I think about

your adventure, the more I want to drive you back home. I don't want your money." He reached up, money in his hand. "Here, take it back. This is a real bad idea."

Gill's objection spurred Clint on. He tipped his hat, waved, and let Millie know it was time to go. What he was about to do was no longer a crazy plan written on a piece of paper. It was real. A feeling of exhilaration swept over him. If his calculations were correct, he'd arrive at the No-Name-Ranch cabin several days ahead of Trace and Troy.

He'd decided to put himself in the same danger with almost the same challenge he'd given his sons. However, he'd assigned himself far less ground to cover, and he planned to stay closer to civilization, just in case. He felt that was fair. His horse would be pulling a trailer containing his metal mustang (he still could not bring himself to call it a wheelchair), feed for the horse, buckets of water, and enough wood for several fires. A custom-made contraption that made it possible for him to dismount his horse was attached behind the saddle. It wasn't a pretty sight, but it worked.

Getting on was difficult but doable. Clint had trained Millie to lie down on command several years ago. With guidance and a boost from the men at the stables and having arms far stronger than any other man his age, he could pull himself up and onto the saddle. The horse would stand up, and off they'd go. In a pinch, he was able to mount the horse on his own using the motorized, elevated seat on his metal mustang – he'd paid dearly to have that particular option invented and installed.

Clint, confident he could go the distance and deal with mounting and dismounting, was concerned mainly with the cold weather. That was by far his greatest challenge. Clouds of semi-frozen breath puffed out from the horse's nostrils as well as his own. For the first time in fifteen years, he was glad his legs had no feeling in them. At least half of him would not mind the below-freezing temperature.

A couple of hours into the ride, his upper body already ached and shivered. Still, he was too stubborn to think about quitting – *Mind over matter. Mind over matter,* his brain chanted silently while his arms drew circles in the air, which brought on a welcomed hint of warmth. Clint and his horse, so instinctively in tune with each other, traveled over rolling, snow-packed hills as one. He reminisced about the good old days before his accident and vowed to keep Millie safe from harm.

CLINT DID NOT PUSH his luck or his horse the first day out. When he came upon a deserted, weather-beaten old shed, he decided to make camp there before darkness set in. It provided shelter from the wind, at least on three sides, and a partial roof over their heads. *Soon I'll be sleeping with my horse, just like the good old days.*

He maneuvered the horse so the trailer parked parallel with the front opening of the shed, adding more protection from whatever might come their way – winter weather or wildlife. He was pleased with himself and his first day on the trail. Everything went according to his plan, and he was able to keep riding from the moment he'd mounted up until now.

He'd pre-thought specific strategies that would allow him to remain in the saddle for hours on end. He was well aware that getting on and off his horse would be the most difficult, strength-stealing aspect of the journey and limited himself to one mount and one dismount per day.

Dismount number one… Reaching behind the saddle, Clint grabbed hold of the lightweight, portable rolling chair bungeed on top of his duffle bag, snapped the chair open, and lowered it to the ground. Next, he tossed down the duffle bag so that it landed close to his chair. Still in the saddle, he used his arms to lift his motionless right leg to the opposite side of the horse and set it by his left leg.

Even though Clint's arms were strong, they needed to rest before beginning the short descent to the ground. He'd practiced his dismounts for years, though until today, there'd always been someone nearby to help if necessary. It would take every ounce of strength and every bit of caution to get down from the horse safely. He could not afford an injury. That could be the end of his journey and, possibly, the end of him.

He wiped the sweat that had formed on his face with the sleeve of his sheepskin coat. He took a deep breath and unrolled his custom-designed contraption consisting of two smooth ropes with three handholds attached to each one. It appeared to be part rope ladder and part rings, like the ones used in gymnastics.

The horse stood utterly still during the entire process. "Almost done, Millie. Then we'll eat and get some sleep." He lowered himself to the ground, twisting his body just enough to settle his butt in the seat of the chair. After catching his breath, he reached up and unhooked the latches on the trailer so his horse could walk freely for a while. Millie turned and stepped directly to the back end of the trailer where two high-grade bales of hay were stored, and helped herself. Watching his horse munch on and shake the hay brought a smile to Clint's face. He loved this horse and would never have considered taking the journey without her or his metal mustang, for that matter. He needed them both.

Damn! His smile faded, and his stomach churned with anxiety. Double damn. He'd been so preoccupied with learning and practicing to mount and dismount the horse, he'd forgotten all about loading and unloading his heavy-duty transportation now sittin' pretty on the trailer. It was no good to him up there. When setting up this part of his challenge, he'd forgotten about using it during the ride.

Back home, all he had to do was push some buttons and flip some switches that were easily within his reach to load and unload the metal mustang from the van. He could do that with his eyes closed, and Gill or Alice was always nearby if he wanted assistance. No buttons or switches here. He had no way to move that mustang from the trailer to the ground. Though not impossible, mounting his horse every morning until he arrived at the cabin would be far more complicated than usual. Clint fought the doubts that threatened to creep in.

Many of the necessities – a cell phone, matches, a large Swiss Army knife, a spoon, a small handgun, and a bag of jerky – were kept in the zippered pockets of his jacket. Duplicates, plus a few flares and his favorite Louis L'Amour book, were in a canvas bag attached to his rolling chair.

He built a small fire a few feet beyond the shed's

open side and added the end of an old piece of timber he'd found in the shed, hoping that would keep the fire burning longer. He'd brought four small cans of stew, the kind with pop-tops, and would eat the first one tonight. After heating it, he took out his only spoon from his coat pocket and dug in. The warm food tasted extra good, and he sighed contentedly. The stew was just what he needed after a successful but exhausting first day.

Of course, it didn't compare to Alice's stew, but out here, it was delicious. He ate every bite, scraping the sides of the can. Now for some real rest. He scooted into the sleeping bag, blew up a small, inflatable pillow, threw one of his Mylar emergency blankets over himself, and whistled for Millie. The horse trotted up and stopped at the shed's opening.

"Come on in. There is plenty of room for you." The horse pawed the ground and seemed restless. She wasn't used to pulling such a heavy load or spending the night away from her stall at Golden Creek Stables. Clint invited her in again, this time with a treat in his hand. "That-a-girl. You're the best horse in the whole world. Sorry about the saddle. In a few days, I'll find someone who can take it off your back."

According to his calculations, he'd spend only two more nights out in the cold, sleeping on the ground. That was doable. The old Clint was back and feeling better about himself than he had in years.

I can't wait to see the look on Alice, Trace, and Troy's faces when I tell them all about the challenge I'd given myself.

That alone was worth any discomfort he might feel along the trail.

Trace figured he was halfway to his final destination, though that was more of a guess than fact. He relived the previous days over and over in his mind as he rode Blackjack along the snow-covered trail. He'd ridden on or near the Sand Creek Massacre Trail from Bosler, through Rock River, and on to Medicine Bow. There, a road sign caught his attention.

If he made an unplanned turn to the west, he'd ride near a town called Hanna. And though he'd no longer have the trail to follow, the railroad tracks also veered to the west, providing him with a landmark of sorts.

"What do you think, Blackjack? Nothing wrong with having a little fun along the way, right?" It didn't matter to him whether he arrived at the cabin first or last, so why not? A decision was made. Was his choice based on the fact that he missed his own sweet Hannah, or had curiosity gotten the better of him? Either way, he made the turn.

Low, rolling hills and a whole lot of wide-open space surrounded the small town. Not much there, though. Nothing worth sharing with Hannah except that he'd seen a town that misspelled her name. Rather than backtrack, he'd push ahead in a westerly direction, keeping the railroad tracks within sight until he came to a trail or dirt road that would take him north.

As luck would have it, he came across a Wyoming Backway headed in the desired direction. But by late afternoon, he regretted his decision to stray from his original plan. It seemed the elevation increased with every step. Up ahead in the distance, it looked like the gently rolling hills became mountains, though he couldn't tell how large or tall they were. Dark clouds covered the peaks. Should he go back to that fork in the road where he'd veered from his original course? That would add a day, maybe two, to his journey. Paralyzed by indecision, he set up camp, fully expecting a wise choice would come to him before daybreak.

THE BRIGHT SUNSHINE gave him the hope and encouragement he needed to continue his trek north. Though covered with several inches of new snow, the uphill, narrow dirt road became visible often enough to assure Trace of its continuing existence. They made good time along this stretch.

With the sun directly overhead, he had a brief *aha* moment and remembered that he had a GPS in one of his coat pockets. Though he'd rather have his phone, this was better than nothing. He dismounted, giving himself and Blackjack a short break to enjoy the sunshine, drink some water, and eat a snack. He switched on the GPS, then waited for a satellite signal to find their location. It didn't take long, but the news wasn't what he'd hoped for.

Horse and rider were definitely on the short side of being halfway there. Trace took a few minutes to adjust to the shocking news and come to grips with the reality of more damn cold days on the snowy trail than he'd planned on. His situation sent shivers up his spine.

"Well, Blackjack, how do you feel about traveling fast for a while?" His horse whinnied and stomped its front hooves. "Okay then. Let's cover some ground while the sun is still shining." They rode like the wind for a couple of miles. Trace, still not remembering all the words, hummed his favorite song, *Fly Like an Eagle* by the Steve

Miller Band, over and over. His horse finally slowed to a walk with no direction from him.

Due to the surrounding hills, the sun disappeared earlier than expected, though darkness was still several hours away. While enough light remained, Trace would watch for a safe, sheltered location to set up camp for the long, cold night ahead of them. When they came to another flat section along the trail, Blackjack took off in a burst of speed without any signal from Trace. The horse appeared to be having fun as it pranced, crow-hopped a couple of times, even bucked once or twice. Was he playing? Or hungry? He was not frightened or angry. Trace knew this horse well. Either way, it made him laugh. For the moment, they'd be a team out on an old Wild West adventure. "Yee-haw!"

While playing around at a high rate of speed, Trace nearly missed the sign. "Whoa! I think we've found the perfect spot." A campground! Primitive and closed for the winter, they'd have it all to themselves.

With the exact spot chosen, Trace took everything from the horse's back: the saddlebags, one contained food, drinks, and a few small utensils; the other held his one-man backpacking tent, two duffle bags filled with bedding, clothing, and a blanket for Blackjack. And for the first time since the ride began, the saddle came off too. The horse needed a break from carrying the load, and tonight, he would wear his blanket. Tonight would likely be the coldest night of their journey.

Trace removed his waterproof, goose down parka and lined jeans to add another layer of clothing over his long johns. In theory, he'd survive temperatures as low as 45 degrees below zero with the clothes on his back. He had no intention of trying to prove that theory, but if he froze to death, he hoped someone would give L. L. Bean a call and write a negative review. He laughed at his ridiculous thought. But the reality of his situation quickly overshadowed his humorous moment. *Shake it off,* he told himself. *There's no turning back now, and I've got work to do.*

The next task on Trace's mental to-do list was to build a fire. A big one. He found plenty of kindling close by but needed to widen his search for large sticks and logs. Conserving fuel for the fire was not on tonight's agenda; keeping warm was the priority. Dusk was upon them, covering their Wyoming winter world in shades of gray. Visibility was minimal, and Trace heard the anxious squeal coming from his horse before the cause became evident.

Hurrying back, his arms loaded down with medium-sized deadfall, he saw them: three scrawny coyotes in a standoff with Blackjack. The horse could hold his own with these three wild, likely hungry canines, but he didn't want him to suffer any injury, no matter how slight it might be. He could shoot the coyotes. He had a gun in his pocket, but he couldn't bring himself to do that, either. Instead, he shot a round into the air. That got their attention, and they quickly disappeared into the darkness, though not empty-handed. One of the bags containing most of Trace's food went with them. Damn!

With many miles to go, how would he keep up his strength without nourishment? He still had a few granola bars and a small pouch of dried fruit, so he wouldn't starve, but he'd become weak, and his ability to keep his body warm would diminish. He craved some protein, not only for its taste but also for the critical calories it provided. He'd give anything for a hot, juicy burger right now. Would his craving drive him to hunt? He'd never been a hunter, which had disappointed his dad, but this was different. He wouldn't shoot a living creature for sport, but for food, maybe.

Not that many meals were out walking around in the dark. Maybe a deer, but Trace couldn't bring himself to take one's life just to get a meal or two. *Hannah would approve of my thought.* And that brought a smile to his face. No, it would have to be something small like a rabbit or a squirrel, or— "Son of a gun," he whispered. Moving slowly, silently, he removed the small pistol from his pocket. A black squirrel ran down one pine tree and then up another. It seemed to focus its attention on Blackjack. Trace waited patiently for it to come a little closer. When it did, he squeezed the trigger. BANG! The horse backed up, the squirrel fell, and Trace sprinted forward toward his kill. He picked up the dead squirrel and laid the nearly unrecognizable carcass near the fire ring with no fear of it spoiling until his fire was ready. After all, the air temperature was colder than the interior of a refrigerator.

He built a good fire and began searching for the only knife he'd brought with him. It had a sharp blade just right for skinning and gutting the squirrel. Once the wood burned down to white-hot coals, that tiny bit of meat would be ready to cook. Trace had heard that it would taste like chicken – every unknown piece of meat tasted like chicken – though that might have been a rumor or an old wives' tale. Anyway, that was the plan, and it would have worked had he found the knife. It must have been in the bag the coyotes confiscated.

He cooked that gut-filled, furry carcass anyway. It was dreadful. It took only one bite of the charred hunk of flesh for his meat craving to disappear completely. He went to bed hungry with a bad taste in his mouth.

A lice smiled, knowing that she was on her way to see Clint. She couldn't wait to prepare some delicious, home-cooked meals and help him get ready for Christmas while he waited for his sons to arrive. Finally, the joy of the holiday season found its way into her heart.

She'd sent Hannah and Ivy their plane tickets, and they would soon follow. A feeling of relief simmered gently through her entire body like fresh apple cider warming on the stove. Life was good again.

The Ford Explorer's heater kept her nice and warm as she sang along with the Christmas tunes coming from the radio. *Winter Wonderland* played when, as if on autopilot, her vehicle turned down the Golden Creek Stables' driveway where they kept their horses just a few miles from their home. Alice laughed. Her absent-minded mistake was forgotten and quickly replaced with a smile and her affection for their horses. "I'll just give them a few treats and a nose rub and be on my way." She had plenty of time to catch her flight departing from the Denver International Airport.

"Howdy, Mrs. McAllister. What brings you here?" Gill asked, appearing surprised. Typically, she rarely came to the stables without Clint.

"Just stopped by to visit with our horses. I'm on my way to Wyoming to meet my husband."

"Well, ma'am. Your horse is here. I'll bring her right out."

"Bring them both out, if you wouldn't mind."

Gill stopped in his tracks, turned, and said, "Mr. McAllister's horse isn't here."

"What? Why? That's not possible," she said as she watched Gill hurry toward the barn. The wrangler must be mistaken. Clint never loaned his horse out for others to ride. He was the only one allowed on Millie's back. The horse had to be here. Where else could it be?

Gill returned with Blondie, Alice's mare. He kicked at the dirt and stared at the ground avoiding eye contact with Mrs. McAllister.

"What's going on, Gill?" she asked, her intuition telling her there was something terribly wrong.

"I sort of loaned your husband my truck and my two-horse gooseneck trailer. Said he had something special he had to do. And it was a secret. I told him it wasn't a good idea and all, but it's Mr. McAllister and… well, I ended up helping him. We hooked up the trailer, then we loaded up *both* horses, if you know what I mean."

She gave the wrangler a knowing nod. Yes, she knew exactly what he meant. "You're sure about that?"

"Look over there," he pointed toward the far end of a long line of stalls. "See? That's where he parked his van."

That was his van. "Why in the world would he do that? He was getting ready to board an airplane."

"It's not my place to question Mr. McAllister."

"I understand. Do passenger planes transport horses?"

"I wouldn't know, ma'am. That's never come up for me."

Bewildered, Alice frowned with concern. She'd check back with Gill later to demand more details, but for now, she needed to get to the airport. "Okay. Well, Merry Christmas. Take good care of my horse. I'll be gone for over a week."

"Will do."

THE PLANE SLAMMED DOWN HARD onto the runway, then seemed as if it would never come to a stop. Alice didn't need that extra tension. She trembled, her nerves already on edge after discovering that her husband had lied to her and embarked on a mysterious adventure. *What was he up to now?* His original plan was unfit for a man with his disability. Maybe his new plan would be safer. She hoped that was the case.

Alice scoured the small area at the only baggage carousel, expecting to see Ivy waiting with her luggage. Her plane was scheduled to arrive first, but there was no sign of her. Not that she knew what Ivy looked like. Still, there was not one young woman in the area. Where could she be? The coffee shop, of course. That made more sense. They'd need to wait for Hannah, and her plane wouldn't arrive for another two hours.

At the coffee shop, she saw only two men who appeared to be airport employees. Where was Ivy? After checking outside and in the ladies' room, Alice determined she wasn't anywhere. Oh, dear. Had she changed her mind about coming? Maybe her flight was delayed. Alice, tugging her carry-on along, walked over to the airline's information booth.

"Excuse me. Can you tell me when flight 521 from Billings will arrive?"

The woman behind the counter looked at her,

surprised. "That flight was right on schedule. Landed several hours ago."

Maybe Ivy missed her flight. "Thank you. When will the next flight from Billings arrive?"

"Tomorrow. Same time. Is there something wrong, ma'am?"

She had given the gals driving directions from the airport to the cabin at the No-Name-Ranch in the event that her flight was delayed. Would Ivy rent a car and drive herself out to the cabin? Surely, if that were the case, she'd have waited for Hannah. Alice's patience was nearly exhausted. "Yes, something is terribly wrong. Can you please check the manifest to see if Ivy Radcliff was on that flight?"

"Sorry, no can do. It's against FAA Policy. I could lose my job if I did something like that." The woman paused, then leaned in close to Alice and whispered, "I can't give you information about a passenger, but I could tell you if I saw her. There weren't many women on that flight. Can you describe Ivy?"

Alice's frustration reached an all-time high, at least for today. "No, not really. All I know is that she's a young woman in her late twenties, probably pretty."

"In my estimation, all the women on that flight were well over forty-five."

She got her answer. "Okay, thanks." A heavy sigh

escaped from her lungs. Ivy was not on that flight. Did she need to worry or be angry? She called Ivy's cell number to find out, but no one answered. Such a frustrating beginning, and now her only option was to wait for Hannah. Perhaps she'd spoken with Ivy and could shed some light on her absence. With time to spare, Alice went ahead and loaded her luggage into the rental car she'd arranged for, then headed back to the coffee shop.

Midway into her second cup of strong, hot coffee, Hannah's plane taxied up to the gate. Alice stood, prepared to greet her and anxious to put her holiday plan in motion. She observed each passenger, one by one, as they entered the waiting area. She'd met Hannah before and knew exactly what she looked like. No! No! No! Hannah was not on the plane.

No doubt about it, Alice was angry. Where were these two women that her sons had chosen to be their wives? How dare her future daughters-in-law not show up, or even call, after all she'd done. Then a different reality dawned on her.

Something unexpected must have happened to both of them. Her worry list just got longer. She dialed Ivy's cell phone first. It rang, but no one answered. When she called Hannah, it sounded like someone picked up, but all she heard was static. No cell service? The price one pays for living far from the *maddening* crowd.

She doubted the cabin had a landline unless Clint had managed to set something up recently. With all he had to think about, that was unlikely. Even if he'd been able to pull that off, she didn't have the number. She sat in her rental vehicle feeling paralyzed, unsure what course of action to take and questioned the wisdom of her plan.

Clint. How would he react when she showed up at the cabin's door? If he'd wanted her there, he would have let her come with him. Had she read between the lines incorrectly? Was it, after all, a McAllister Men's Reunion and nothing more?

Is my idea even crazier than Clint's?

SEVENTEEN

TROY

Troy did not need a prize or a reward of any kind. The satisfaction of arriving before his little brother would be enough. He had made terrific time and was well ahead of schedule.

Glancing at the map he carried with him, he faced two choices: he could turn south, ride five miles, and arrive at the cabin several days ahead of Trace, or he could keep going west and check out something on his map labeled Lost Cabin. Those two words intrigued him, and his curiosity won the toss. He hooked up with the Bridger Trail and headed west.

His good luck and his decent traveling days came to an abrupt end. A storm caught him off guard. He never saw it coming. A curtain of white obstructed his visibility, forcing him to travel slowly and stop often to make sure he wasn't about to fall off a cliff. By the time his surroundings came into view, he knew they were in a ravine where the windblown snow was so deep in spots that Gunner was nearly high-centered. The horse panicked and began to twist and squeal.

"Whoa, Gunner," he repeated many times as he dismounted. The horse and rider were in for a unique experience. Troy took a few steps and discovered he did not break through the crunchy snow, as did Gunner. So he grabbed the reins and walked ahead of the horse, speaking calm, encouraging words the entire time and giving those reins and the horse a good strong pull now and then. It was slow going, but eventually, they cleared the snow-packed ravine and found a suitable site to make camp and rest. They were both hungry and exhausted.

The next day, Troy had no trouble finding Lost Cabin but was sorely disappointed. What he found was a couple of vacant houses and one other building that resembled a mansion. It seemed so out of place – a mystery for another day. He'd traveled all this way to see a ghost town and read a few plaques that spoke of legends, skeletons, gold, and death. Lost Cabin was a lost cause.

He'd look it up online and learn about the legends once he returned to civilization. But now, reaching the original destination was once again his priority. He retraced his journey on Bridger Trail for a while, avoiding the ravine, then took a turn to the south, thinking that would be a quicker way to Powder Mesa.

Within an hour, an odd noise caught his attention. It seemed to be some kind of animal sound, though very weak. He stopped for a moment to listen. Was it a bobcat or two? The sounds came from more than one animal. He was sure of that. Troy veered away from the sounds but not due to fear or that it would place Gunner or himself in danger. He just wasn't up to any kind of animal encounter. His interests focused firmly on a warm cabin, a comfy bed, and some real food.

Like it or not, he ended up close enough to see that the source of the sound was not a bobcat but rather a pile of smaller animals. A pile? He blinked and looked again, then dismounted Gunner. The horse backed away from the odd, soft cries. A slight change in airflow brought with it a putrid odor, nearly causing Troy to gag. Putting his gloved hand over his nose and mouth, he stepped close enough to assess the matter he could longer ignore. He counted seven small animals, but only three were alive. *Nope, I do not need this. Dammit.*

The live ones, wet from living out in the elements, shivered, shook, and made small, painful cries. Troy desperately wanted to walk away. He could have, knowing they'd all die in a matter of days, but it broke his heart to see them suffering. He knew what Ivy would do, but he wasn't Ivy. Even so, rather than leave and let nature take its brutal course, Troy surprised himself. He rearranged his items, freeing up one of the sacks for the three living animals. He mounted Gunner and rode away, sack and all.

Traveling would be slow now, no cantering, just walking. His wish to arrive first was no longer possible and would not be granted. So be it.

EIGHTEEN

ALICE

The air was cold and damp, and the sky's color resembled a rainbow trout with flecks of gold. Alice estimated that the sun, partially blocked by thin, gray clouds, would dip below the horizon in less than an hour.

Unable to reach any family members, finding her way to the No-Name-Ranch without Ivy or Hannah seemed to be her only choice. If Clint wasn't happy about her sudden appearance, well, too bad. She was in no mood for a confrontation with him or anyone.

She started the rental car's engine, turned on the heater, and, before pulling out of the airport's parking lot, tapped all the presets on the radio in search of a station. Not much there. Just like the phones, there was lots of static and a little bit of news, but she yearned for music.

Joyful, holiday music. Digging through her large, leather tote bag on the seat beside her, she found her favorite Mannheim Steamroller Christmas CD. On the drive, she sang along with the unique instrumental versions of *Joy to the World, Deck the Halls*, and *Good Kind Wenceslas* until a road sign caught her eye.

Powder Mesa, one mile. Within seconds, she'd turn right on Road B7. She laughed. The street name triggered a silly but brief vision of a bingo game. Then, there it was, the rough dirt road, and she began the final miles of the trip. A nervous but happy excitement danced through her core. She'd be relieved to see Clint even if he was displeased to see her.

Crossing the unexpected railroad tracks was the most challenging part of driving up the rugged, snow-covered dirt road. No, it didn't deserve to be called a road, not even a dirt one. It was more of a rarely used tire-track path. Not wanting to damage the rental vehicle, it was slow going. The snow was several inches deep, and tire tracks from another vehicle or two had already left their mark. Whose vehicles? One of them had better be Gill's truck and trailer.

The road ended at the cabin. Alice saw two vehicles parked on either side of the cabin's door: a Jeep displaying a Colorado license plate and a Suburban. The latter had backed in, its plate out of sight. The truck and trailer Clint supposedly borrowed were nowhere to be seen. Interesting. Then it dawned on Alice that he'd probably driven into town to arrange for food, gifts, and a housecleaner. "So, this is the No-Name-Ranch."

During the early years of their marriage, she'd heard that Clint owned a piece of land in Wyoming, but she'd never seen it and knew next to nothing about it. Until a few weeks ago, she'd forgotten it existed. The cabin, a rustic, old log home, more massive than she expected, was the only house on the ranch property. From her vantage point, it looked like it should be condemned.

Approaching the door, pulling a large piece of luggage with one arm, and grasping a duffle bag with her other hand, she heard laughter, music, and... barking? Yipping? Should she knock? Hell, no. *Ready or not, here I come.*

Loaded down, she kicked at the door with her boot-covered foot hoping the two missing women had generated some of the sounds she'd heard. Alice was ready to give them a piece of her mind for not using their plane tickets, not following her directions, and causing her to worry unnecessarily.

"Alice, you made it! We're all here now," Hannah's words tumbled out with so much exuberance, they curbed the frustration that Alice brought with her.

"Wait 'til you see what we've done," Ivy added, then

took the duffle bag from Alice, freeing her arm while Hannah relieved her of the rolling luggage. The three women embraced, and a commotion followed.

"Oh, my. Who do we have here?" Alice asked, shocked, but delighted.

A small child, a boy, stepped right up to Alice, held out his hand, and said, "My name is Billy." He pointed at Ivy. "She's my mommy."

With wide-open eyes, Alice searched for the right words. "Oh! I guess my earlier question about a pregnancy was overdue – by five or six years. I understand now why you didn't want to talk about it." That didn't come out right, and now she regretted her off-handed comment. He was a sweet little boy, but he was not Troy's son, and she would not bear the title of grandma for someone else's child.

Hannah picked up the awkward slack and introduced the animals. "You already know Oatie, Trace's all-time favorite dog," she said, as Oatie made his way quickly to her.

Alice bent down to pet him. "Hi, Oatie. You're looking good. Who are your other two friends?"

"This is Little Charlie, Oatie's puppy."

Ivy scooped up the remaining dog, a puppy, too, she guessed by its size. "Alice, I'd like you to meet Shadow. She's the Lonely Horse Ranch's only pet."

"Interesting. Troy has never been fond of pets or children or relationships." *What is the matter with me? I've got to adjust my attitude, or Christmas will not be merry.*

Ivy kept quiet, threw on a coat, and went outside to retrieve the remaining items from Alice's rental car. Hannah quickly steered her future mother-in-law to the bedroom where she and Clint would sleep. "We thought you'd like this one. It's the largest bedroom in the cabin."

"This room is lovely. Rustic, but lovely. Oh, my. I didn't know Clint had it in him. He's such an outdoor man; home interior decorating was never his thing. I'm impressed beyond words at what he's accomplished in such a short time."

They found Ivy in the main living room lighting a fire in the large wood stove with the help of one of the pups. It shook its head and thrashed a piece of newspaper like it was a rat. All of Alice's bags were inside, lined up not far from the front door.

"Want a tour?"

Alice was grateful for a distraction from several burning questions now occupying her thoughts. "Sure. That would be nice."

While guiding Alice from room to room, the young women offered suggestions for changes or additions to the cabin. Some could be accomplished right away. Others were more suited for future gatherings. Alice listened and hoped to see Clint napping in one of the rooms, allowing her to check off the main question from her mental list and make the tour complete.

"That's about it. Pretty cool, huh? Lots of potential."

Alice nodded and hugged Hannah. She remembered how they'd connected the first night they met despite the horrific circumstances. And she had to admit that Troy's future bride seemed to have a cheerful, upbeat soul.

"Where is Clint? Did he drive into town for something?"

The gals exchanged puzzled glances as if she'd asked a trick question.

"Maybe?" said Hannah, her brief answer permeated with skepticism, or was that secrecy. "He wasn't here when we arrived. I wouldn't blame him if he'd left for a while."

"The place was disgusting with plenty of evidence it had been occupied by a variety of critters." Ivy didn't mince words.

Alice scanned the room. Yes, she knew exactly what Ivy was referring to, but everything looked all right. She saw no disgusting evidence of critters.

"I think planning and coordinating this reunion and Christmas celebration at the cabin has taken its toll on Clint. So, in a way, it makes sense that he'd seek out some help and a comfortable, clean room in town. I'm sure he'll pull in any minute." Alice prayed she was right.

"Let's hope he does. He couldn't have stayed anywhere close, though, because there isn't anything nearby. No food or lodging." Hannah's statement derailed Alice's thinking, and her moment of optimism vanished quicker than water down a well-working drain.

MAC 'N CHEESE & MYSTERIES, POACHERS & THE CABIN

lice put on her coat, hat, and gloves. "I'm stepping out for some fresh air. I won't be gone long."

Alone with her thoughts and worries, more questions popped up. What would Clint be driving when he finally did pull in? The specially equipped rental van they'd arranged for or the stable manager's truck? A sudden realization nearly knocked her down. No! He couldn't possibly drive any vehicle not designed for his disability. And where was his horse, Millie?

She called Clint's cell phone, then Trace's, and finally Troy's. None of the calls went through. It seems all three of her men were not within cell service range. Or was she the one out of range? Either way, she felt out of touch. Alice tried calling their home phone in Colorado, hoping one of the men might have left a message on their landline. That call went through, but no message had been recorded.

Desperate, she called the Natrona Airport just outside of Casper, hoping to confirm that he'd landed there safely back on December 10th according to his original plan. That was a long shot and made no sense, especially after hearing that he'd borrowed Gill's truck and trailer, but she had to give it a try.

The woman who'd helped her earlier that afternoon was still at work. "I remember you. Did you ever find your girls?"

"I did, thank you. Now I'm looking for my husband. He would have flown in on December 10th, and he might've had a horse with him."

"I can tell you this, you've made my day interesting." It came as no surprise when the woman was unable to share any passenger information with her, but she assured Alice that no horses landed there, ever.

"Okay. Well, thank you again for your help."

If Clint hadn't flown, someone must have driven him. Or maybe he'd gone somewhere else and had no intention of arriving at this old cabin. She knew he'd suffered from depression occasionally, though he never acknowledged such a weakness. Did that play a role in his absence?

Shivering from the cold, the fear, and the emptiness,

she returned to the warmth of the cabin, hoping to shed some light on her darkening thoughts. *Clint had no way of knowing that I'm worried sick about him because he thinks I'm at home oblivious to his alternate plan – whatever that might be.*

"SOMETHING SMELLS DELICIOUS IN HERE," Alice said.

"Mommy made my favorite dinner: mac and cheese, hot dogs, and popcorn. She said there's enough for everybody." The little boy beamed with his good news.

Alice stared down at Billy, thinking he must be the child qualifying her for the unwanted title of grandmother. Next to him sat three dogs smiling up at her, and for a few moments, her worry took a back seat to the four adorable faces.

"Let's eat," Ivy said. They gathered around a large rectangular table that could comfortably seat eight and passed around a platter of hot dogs and buns and two bowls, one filled with macaroni and cheese and the other piled high with popcorn. "Dig in!"

"How come you didn't take a hot dog, Miss Hannah? Don't you like 'em?"

"Out of the mouths of babes," said Ivy, smiling at Billy's sweet innocence.

Alice's curious eyes turned toward Hannah, awaiting her answer.

"I'm sure they're delicious, Billy. I just don't eat meat." She whispered the word meat.

I guess she's not so perfect after all, thought Alice. A vegetarian and a cattleman? How could a pairing like that possibly stand the test of time?

"Just so you know, Alice, there were several FedEx boxes on the porch when we got here. We opened them, hope you don't mind, and found a few food items, pots and dishes, and some bedding," said Ivy.

"And we'll go to town tomorrow to shop for some food and other necessities from a *real* store," Hannah chimed in. "You should have seen this place when we arrived. We stood and stared, not knowing what to do first."

"Actually, we were shocked at the condition of the cabin," Ivy interjected. "So, we assessed the immediate needs and headed off to Powder Mesa to shop for more food and cleaning supplies, which was a total bust. There were no stores, none."

"But we were able to grab a bag of junk food, a broom, some sponges, and a bottle of liquid cleaner at a gas station on the way back. We added those items to the hot dogs, buns and popcorn that Ivy brought with her. Although our first shopping trip was very disappointing, we managed to clean things pretty well with our limited supplies." Hannah was all smiles now, likely glad the conversation had moved on from her self-imposed diet restrictions.

Alice nodded and frowned at the same time. "When did you both get here?"

"The day you said start packing, we did. I called Ivy and, to make a long story short, we came to the conclusion that we each needed to drive. Flying was out of the question. We had some very active and lovable baggage that we could not leave behind or take on a plane."

"I waited at the airport for both of you. When you didn't show up, I was worried sick, wondering what might have happened. Now, I think I know. You took off before your airline tickets arrived."

When Alice saw the shocked and remorseful looks on the two young women's faces, she knew her assumption was correct. She could put aside the initial anger she'd felt and forgive them.

Billy broke the silence. "Good thing we came early, huh?"

Alice's face softened as she looked at the small boy. "Yes, arriving early was a very good thing."

They'd come early, had been here several days, and

neither of the gals had seen Clint. That information brought a sudden pain to her chest and drained the blood from her head, causing a swirling, dizzy feeling. "Ladies, if you'll excuse me, I need to lie down for a while. Thank you for everything you've done." On her way to the bedroom, she rubbed each dog's ears and gave Billy a kiss on his forehead.

TWENTY
CLINT

Two nights of sleeping on the ground had taken their toll. Sitting up, Clint groaned and stretched his arms, unable to relieve or ignore the soreness that seemed to radiate from every inch of his upper body.

Though his lower body gave no signals, he knew it was time to eliminate all the water he'd swallowed last night. He quickly stuffed his bedding, food, water bottles, and medication back into the duffle bag. Then, dragging himself several feet from both his fold-up, rolling chair and the bag, he took care of business.

He found Millie helping herself to breakfast, then lapping water from one of her buckets. At last, the sun poked its head above the horizon, announcing a cloudless sky. It was time to hook up, mount up, and take full advantage of this nearly perfect traveling day. Clint knew what to do, though none of it was easy. At almost every turn, some kind of improvisation was required. Lifting the duffle bag was difficult, and getting the rolling chair in place would be downright tricky, to say the least.

With the metal mustang not an option, he'd be mounting Millie the old-fashioned way again today. That was exhausting and demanding but doable. The horse lay down and remained down until Clint tipped forward from his chair, grasped a stirrup, and pulled himself horizontally across the horse's belly as if rope climbing. When his hands reached the saddle horn, he performed one final hoist, which left him lying partially across the saddle on his stomach like a dead man but holding on tight. There he rested for a while before grabbing hold of his duffle bag and the folding chair, and the last bit of mounting acrobatics took place.

"Okay, Millie. UP!" The horse stood, though not easily, and Clint pushed and pulled himself into a sitting position. Exhausted, he rested again. The process hadn't seemed so darn difficult in the past.

Only one task remained, and then they could be on their way. From high in the saddle, Clint guided the horse around the trailer several times, then backed her up so that she stood between the trailer's two rails. Once in place, Clint reached down and attached them to the special harness the horse wore for this trip. From beginning to end, the whole process took a hell of a lot of time, strength, and patience for both the rider and the horse.

"You know, Millie, I've said this before, and I'll say it again. Without you, I'd never have considered making this journey. And now that we've experienced every task we'll need to accomplish each day, the rest is downhill. What's that saying Alice likes? Oh, yeah. Wash. Rinse. Repeat. We've got this!"

The sun shone down brightly though Clint felt certain the temperature never rose above freezing. Sometime past noon, a few clouds gathered to the north. All in all, other than cold, this was a peaceful, pleasant day. The slow rocking motion of the horse and the clopping of its hooves on the hard, sometimes snow-packed ground had a lulling effect on Clint, and he came within seconds of falling asleep. If Millie hadn't come to an abrupt stop, he probably would have.

"Well, my friend, I'd hoped all the rivers and streams would be dry or frozen solid this time of year. Seems I might have been wrong about that. At least it's not very wide, and it can't be very deep." Clint could not avoid making this crossing if he wanted to reach the cabin before his sons did. Glancing east and west at the small, meandering river, he decided this was as good a place as any to cross. He slapped the reins lightly and said, "Take her slow and easy, Millie."

The river appeared to be frozen. The trailer was tall enough to keep the metal mustang above the few spots where river water flowed over the ice; only occasional sprays and drops splashed on it. They had only ten or fifteen feet to go – so far, so good – when Millie broke through the ice and her front legs collapsed. The horse panicked, screeching and struggling while Clint hung on for dear life.

The trailer carrying his metal mustang thrashed and clanked, but all he could think about was calming and steadying his horse and making it to dry land in one piece. It happened so fast; it felt unreal. Millie found her footing and managed to stand back up. It ended just as quickly as it had begun. *Thank God.* But now, both the horse and rider were wet. So much for their pleasant, peaceful day.

Looking back at the river, Clint noticed how the water's movement had changed in places after the collapse of its icy surface. A cargo of slush kept the flow to a slow trickle. His thoughts quickly turned to the topic of hypothermia. The cold was deadly enough, but now that he was wet, hypothermia would set in much faster.

With the freezing temperature, his wet horse was in danger too. He didn't know what to do about this new hurdle that slowed him down and made the journey uncomfortable and more prolonged than it should be. They hadn't traveled nearly far enough to call it a day, but there was no other choice.

"Millie, we need to find some type of shelter right away. We won't be picky. Just about anything will do."

Damn! The wind kicked up. The chill factor that came with it was unbearable. Finding protection from the elements was a *must* and far more critical than the desire to merely feel comfortable. He was so close to proving to his family, his deceased ancestors, and the world that Clint McAllister was a strong, vigorous man who could accomplish anything. He wouldn't give up. Failure was not an option.

A PAINFUL HOUR PASSED, one of the longest in Clint's life. The cold – and he had to admit fear – numbed him. His thoughts turned dark. The unthinkable had entered his mind, and he was powerless to shake it off. *The only thing worse than lifeless legs was no legs at all.*

He pushed on mostly for the sake of his horse. When Millie began to trot, he wondered why. He hadn't given a signal for the horse to pick up speed. Perhaps she thought she'd be warmer trotting. The horse might have been warmer, but Clint wasn't. The movement added to the wind chill effect. Then, right before his eyes, the reason for the horse's change in speed and direction appeared.

A cave. As they moved closer, Clint noticed that it was more of an overhanging cliff than a cave, but they'd have a roof over their heads and an arc-shaped, rocky, dirt wall that would block out the wind. They might live to see another day. That was all he needed to get himself back on the right track.

He began the arduous tasks of dismounting, unpacking, and setting up for the night though it was only mid-afternoon. To continue traveling today would be foolish. Their shelter was large enough for Millie to stand or lay on her side, yet small enough that the heat from a fire would dry Clint's clothing and the horse's hair and offer just enough warmth to keep them alive.

Even within this adequate setup, he worried about his legs and hoped not too much harm had come to them. Of course, he felt nothing, so it was difficult to know. The circulation in his lower half wasn't all that great on a good day, but today did not fall into the "good day" category. For now, not wanting to make his bedding damp, he sat on the ground close to the fire, rubbing his legs vigorously. What else could he do?

TWENTY-ONE

A nother day had passed, and none of the women's cell phones rang, chimed, or whistled to announce an incoming call. They could no longer chalk up the lack of calls to having no cell service. Yesterday, Alice's call to her own home in Colorado went through just fine.

They all felt concern for their men, and the absence of communication did not help. Troy and Trace were each on a long, dangerous journey, but so far, the women thought the weather along their approximate routes, though cold, remained mostly sunny, though they didn't know for sure. The depth of the snow already on the ground was unknown too.

Clint's whereabouts was a total mystery. The man was still missing in action. Or was he up to something he didn't want Alice or anyone else to know about? It wouldn't be the first time. *Thank God he's not riding through Wyoming on horseback like his sons.*

Clint, Troy, and Trace each had a macho side, and that, according to Alice's way of thinking, was the only excuse for Clint to invent and for her sons to take on this foolish challenge. They said there'd be few opportunities to make phone calls. As frustrated as the women were, there did not seem to be anything they could do yet. So, they sat around the table creating an extensive shopping list. Tomorrow they'd drive to Casper and spend some time in Walmart and Target.

Noticing Little Charlie staring at the front door, Hannah said, "I'm going to take Oatie and the pup out for a walk." Slipping into her warm coat, boots, gloves, and hat, she looked back at Shadow. "Does she want to come too?"

Ivy's pup jumped down from her lap but then sat at her feet. "Thanks. I guess not. Maybe next time."

Alice jerked when her phone rang. It was the first call she'd received since she'd left home. She took a deep breath and steadied herself, hoping it was Clint and not a robo sales call or the highway patrol, or— "Hello?"

"Hey, Mom. I'm just checking in," Troy said, though the connection was a bit garbled.

Thank God! With wide-open, excited eyes, she put a

finger to her lips, sending a signal to Ivy and Billy for silence. "What a wonderful surprise. How's your journey going?"

"Okay, I suppose. It's darn cold, and I could use a hot meal and a hot shower. How's everything at home?"

At a loss for words, what could she say? She was never good at lying, especially to family. "Well, I'm not home at the moment." That was the truth. Then Shadow yipped.

"Did I just hear a dog?"

"Oh, that's probably just something on the TV."

"You're watching TV?"

"No, I'm not watching it. I'm, uh, in the electronic section of the store, and there are lots of TVs turned on." That was a full-blown lie. She must change the subject before her lies traveled beyond the point of no return. She walked to the other side of the room to distance herself a bit from any additional sounds that might come from Billy, the dog, or Ivy.

"Mom, have you heard from Trace?" he shouted. The connection faltered. The sound of wind whooshed in Alice's ear.

She yelled back. "No, and neither has Hannah. She's beside herself, though hopeful, assuming like the rest of us he's merely out of cell range."

Billy covered his ears with his small hands. "Is Grandma Alice mad?" he whispered.

Ivy shook her head.

"But you've spoken with Dad, right?" Troy continued.

"I was hoping maybe you'd heard from—"

Crackling static added to the phone's whooshing noise. "Troy?" More static. "If you can hear me, call Ivy." Crackle. Hiss. Nothing.

TWENTY-TWO

CLINT

Clint's initial calculations led him to believe he'd arrive at the cabin – yesterday. Already, the journey had taken too long. With each passing hour, his physical strength reached a new all-time low. He'd counted on the help of the metal mustang. Without it, pulling himself on the hard, icy ground was his only way forward. The sleeves on his coat had worn thin from that unavoidable activity adding to his discomfort.

He veered farther and farther from civilization to avoid being seen slithering on the ground and to reduce any temptation of giving up on meeting his challenge. Too proud to seek assistance, even if there was an opportunity to do so, Clint kept pushing forward.

In many ways, however, he'd been lucky the first three days except for the quick dunk in the river. That luck empowered him emotionally and built his confidence, though not his strength, to a level that allowed him to do away with his cumbersome seatbelt. He didn't need it anymore. Knowing he'd likely reach the cabin later today, he was determined to enjoy the beautiful morning. The air was still, and the sun shone brightly, elevating his spirit. But as noon approached, ominous clouds billowed up overhead, and snow began to fall, limiting his vision.

Looking to the west, the direction he needed to be traveling right now, he hoped to find some type of structure where they could wait for the storm to pass. Even a stand of trees would be better than nothing. The snowflakes multiplied until the sky and the air around Clint became an opaque veil of white. The sun could no longer warm him or guide him. It had disappeared entirely.

"Whoa there, Millie." Should he go blindly forward or stand still and freeze? His options were bleak, and he paused in the hushed stillness. If he'd been closer to his destination, he might have enjoyed the serenity that falling snow could bring, but honestly, at the moment, he didn't know where he was.

He chose to keep moving. "And you're going to lead

the way for a while, Millie. So, if we—" Sounds interrupted his words. He heard a noise, and it was coming their way. Another horse? No, more than one. Wild? Wyoming had herds of wild horses. The stillness retreated, the wind howled, making the approaching sounds harder to identify. Clint listened. Maybe there were riders on those horses. That could be a good thing. They might know of a nearby shelter of some sort.

"Who in their right mind would be out riding these hills in a snowstorm?" He laughed. "Don't answer that," he said, patting his horse on the neck. Didn't matter. He had a gun and would use it if necessary. This wasn't his first rodeo.

Two men rode up and positioned themselves on either side of him. Clint took their posturing to be an act of intimidation. Though dressed in shabby winter clothing, they looked like men straight out of *Deliverance*. Dirty, ragged, and in need of a shave. He wondered how they'd describe his appearance.

At this point, he was no knight in shining armor either. If they knew the area well and could help him get to a town or at least to some shelter despite the whiteout, he'd overlook their rag-tag appearance and be courteous. *Maybe God sent these rough-looking riders my way. Who knows? Besides, beggars can't be choosers.*

"What do we have here?" one of the men shouted over the howling wind.

"Looks like an old man's dog and pony show."

"Hey, fellas. I'm not that old, and as you can see, there is no dog with me." They'd pushed one of Clint's buttons, and he couldn't ignore their disrespectful comment. His adrenaline flowed, and the macho rancher's ego emerged more potent than ever. "Do I see a dead antelope on the back of your horse? Antelope season ended on October 20th, and if I'm not mistaken, it's December." He felt a rush of anger mixed with anxiety. Game violations did not sit well with him. These guys were poachers, no doubt about it. Clint drew his pistol from his coat pocket and aimed it at one of the men.

"Hey, old man. Don't you be pointing a gun at my brother."

Clint grinned. "Okay. How's this?" He aimed at the man who had spoken.

"Thanks, Darrell. Thanks a lot." The poacher brothers argued, but they also drew their guns.

Two guns against one. Clint didn't like those odds, but it seemed too late to back down. He'd have to outsmart them. "I don't usually shoot fellow humans, but if push comes to shove, a man's gotta do what a man's gotta do. Just so you know, I'm well aware that if a gunfight takes place, I won't survive. But neither will one of you."

"He's bluffin'. He don't wanna die today."

"Go ahead. Call my bluff, and then you'll know which of you winds up dead on the ground in a mist of crimson. However, I'd rather negotiate."

The brothers exchanged smug looks. The one named Darrell smirked and said, "I don't think so, old man."

Clint bit his tongue, controlling his urge to lash out. "What is it you fellas want?"

"What do we want, Luke?" Maniacal laughter mingled with the turbulent, snow-filled air.

"Everything. Yeah, we want everything, especially your pretty, four-footed friend." They continued to laugh and fired off a few shots toward the darkening sky. "Get off your horse, old man."

That presented a problem. Until now, the poachers had no idea just how vulnerable Clint was. He sat firm.

"Are you deaf? Get off the damn horse!"

Clint never took kindly to demands.

No one tells me what to do. He was determined to fire his gun and take one of them out when Darrell reached over and yanked him from his horse. His only weapon flew through the air, and he hit the frozen ground hard, lying in pain and unable to move.

Fortunately, they were stupid men and thought he'd merely suffered a temporary injury from the fall. Unfortunately, they were also evil men. Witnessing Clint's vulnerabilities, regardless of their cause or severity, Darrell – now off his horse – picked up Clint's gun and unhooked Millie from the trailer.

"Take my wheelchair. It's worth a lot more than my old horse." He hoped they'd fall for his lie. Millie was priceless to him. In his lifetime, he'd already lost one horse due to his own stupidity. He could not go through that again. He'd lose all his willpower and motivation if he lost this magnificent horse too.

The men saw the fold-up chair tied to the back of the saddle. "Right, like we'd have any use for that hunk of junk."

"Not that one, the one on the trailer." Clint pointed to his metal mustang.

"That big hunk of metal is a wheelchair?" Luke scratched his beanie-covered head. "You're lying. That's a snowmobile. We're not that stupid," he said, getting off his horse and walking over to the trailer. With much huffing, groaning, and cussing, he finally managed to push the wheelchair contraption off the trailer. He stared at it blankly, then started pushing buttons randomly, hoping it would do something. "How the hell does this piece of junk work?" he shouted, turning on Clint.

"Leave it," Darrell said as he rummaged through Clint's duffle bag, taking only the containers of pills. "The horse, his gun, and these will do." Grinning like a crazed Cheshire cat, he shook the small containers like they were maracas. "We need to get going. Weather's gettin' worse."

They had no use for either of his wheelchairs or his duffle bag, but they were dead set on taking his horse. Clint offered the poachers one of the family's ranches if they'd just leave the horse. His survival depended on Millie, plus the fact she was right up there with his love for Alice, Trace, and Troy.

Darrell, wearing a cowboy hat with a Denver Bronco muffler stretched over the top and tied under his chin, scoffed. "You expect us to believe that you'd give us a ranch? You think we're fools?"

Actually, he did, but he kept that thought safely inside his head. Too busy stealing the few items he had, the poacher brothers had put away their guns. If only he had another weapon or the use of his legs, he could've taken these thugs down in spite of his advanced age.

"If you were some rich, old cowboy, you would not be out here in this God-forsaken weather, risking what's left of your pitiful life. Nope. You're just a crazy, old man. No one's gonna miss you."

From the ground, looking up, Clint took one more

shot at negotiating with these lowlifes. "I have access to several large ranches. One of them is nearby. Just a few miles north of the Powder Mesa road sign. I'll trade that for my horse."

"Right, like that's ever gonna happen. What's your name, old man?"

"Clint. Clint McAllister." Under normal circumstances, he wouldn't divulge personal information, but nothing about today was normal, and he seemed to have no other options. His back was against the wall.

Darrell held Clint's horse by the reins while Luke mounted his own horse. Before he could pass those reins over to Luke so he could mount up, too, Millie bucked and reared up, then kicked him hard in the side. Darrell shrieked like a rabbit stuck in a barbed-wire fence.

Clint hoped Millie's kick had cracked a rib or two and felt an ounce of satisfaction in Darrell's injury. *Serves him right!*

Millie put up a magnificent fight. She would not leave Clint's side willingly. Luke grabbed and firmly held Millie's reins while his partner, bent over and limping, struggled to mount his horse. While Clint lay helpless on the ground, the two thieves whooped and hollered like rodeo champions as they galloped away with their newly acquired stolen property.

Clint's challenge had evolved from difficult to

impossible right before his eyes. If only he'd worn the damn seatbelt, he might still be sitting tall on Millie's back right now. Instead, he lay on the frozen ground thinking only of what would become of his horse. He felt certain the poacher brothers treated animals even worse than they treated people. His heart broke as he watched the horse buck and rear until it was out of sight.

A flash of unexpected sunshine blinded him for a moment. It brought him back to his senses and thoughts of survival. He'd be no good to his horse, dead. Though the lightweight, folding wheelchair was long gone, as was his horse, he still had the metal mustang. Luckily, that idiot, Luke, hadn't been able to figure it out, so Clint could use it now. Yet another challenge reared its ugly head. How would he get on the damn thing? He'd never done that from lying prone on the ground. That scenario hadn't come up before, yet here it was. He'd always mounted that ride from his folding wheelchair or with the help of Gill or Alice.

Needing some help, he searched his pockets for his phone. Would he make a call? Give up? Let his family know he'd failed? He never found his phone, so his questions went unanswered. With no options at hand, he struggled, dragging and pulling himself along the ground with his arms, and then up onto the machine. He must succeed. He must go now before the storm circles back around and hits full blast.

CLINT MISSED the sounds of his horse: the whinnying, the snorting, her hooves meeting with the ground, everything. Though thankful for his metal mustang, the sound of its engine did little more than remind him of his disability and cause his head to ache. Not sure of his exact location, he convinced himself that traveling in a westerly direction would bring him close to his destination sometime tomorrow. With no trailer to pull, no tall horse to mount and dismount each day, he might arrive sooner.

His newly regained positive attitude faded with the oncoming darkness as he watched the purple-black clouds consume the sky. He'd keep a steadfast lookout for cover. He'd found various forms of primitive shelter on the first three nights of his journey. Would his lucky streak continue tonight? He'd always heard "third time's a charm," and, as nickel-size snowflakes began to fall, he hoped this fourth night would follow suit.

Spotting a structure off in the distance – a blur, really – he headed toward it, hoping it was more than a big rock or a small hill. A real building would be a godsend. The snow fell thick and silent as he prayed for shelter.

Clint blinked. Were his eyes playing tricks on him? Was he dreaming? Or was this sight before him, his heaven? There stood a farmhouse. He drove his metal mustang closer and stopped a few feet from the front door.

He hollered, "Hello? Anybody home?" He pressed the button on the mustang that produced a car-horn noise. Nothing. No response. The place, though intact, appeared deserted. Maybe it was only occupied in the summer. That made sense.

He maneuvered the mustang closer and sideways so his hand could reach the door. He tried to open it, but it was either locked or stuck. He drove around the entire building but found no other way to enter. He had to get inside. It was nearly dark, and several inches of new snow covered the ground already.

Returning to that sideways position, he pushed on the door with every bit of strength left in his arms. No luck. What could he do? Rodeo! It was time for a rodeo. He backed the mustang up, revved the engine, turned the gas lever as far as it would go, and yelled, "Yee-Haw!"

The wooden doorjamb splintered on impact, loosening the lock, and the door flew open. Clint, still riding the mustang, found himself in the middle of a small kitchen-living room area complete with a wood stove.

"Now, that's the way to do it."

Clint looked around and marveled at his good luck. Though dusty and covered with cobwebs, a pile of logs and a sealed bag containing several starter pellets sat next to an old woodstove. Without wasting any time, he pushed the door closed while still sitting on the machine and lit a fire. He maneuvered the mustang back up against the door, counting on its weight to keep the wind from blowing it open or any intruders from entering. Ever since the incident with Luke and Darrell, concerns about intruders were right up there with the dangers associated with the weather.

If he had to be stranded in a snowstorm between Casper and Powder Mesa, Wyoming, this small, rustic farmhouse wasn't a bad place to be. Confident he was safe and secure for the time being, he slid off his machine, tossed his duffle bag closer to the fire, and scooted himself in the same direction. The fire roared, warming the cozy room as he unpacked his bedding and ate a can of stew. He'd figure out tomorrow when tomorrow arrived.

For now, he had hope as long as the wood piled beside the stove held out. Conservation of nature's fuel was key. He let the fire burn down, banked a few small logs, and nurtured it throughout the night.

Unavoidably, the day's exertion and physical toll caught up with him, and his eyes closed. As sleep approached, a few final thoughts drifted in and out of his mind. More than anything, he wanted to spend Christmas with his family. Would he find a way to meet his challenge? Would he make it to the No-Name-Ranch? Hell yes, as long as he didn't meet his maker first.

TWENTY-THREE

ALICE

They'd taken Ivy's Suburban, the largest of their vehicles. Now, on the trip back to the cabin, every spare inch of space was filled with food, more decorations, a small flat-screen television, a CD player, and some DVDs and CDs. Ivy had insisted on purchasing plenty of sparkling water, and Hannah was equally insistent on bringing back several bottles of champagne. To call it cozy was an understatement.

The pets greeted the shoppers with wagging tails and plenty of barking. Billy took charge of keeping an eye on them while the women unloaded the SUV.

"Come on in, Billy. Round up your furry friends."

"Can't we stay out a little longer? We're all catching

snowflakes in our mouths. Oatie is really good at it. But Shadow and Little Charlie are learnin' fast. Watch this."

Ivy not only watched the four opened mouths tipped up to the sky but caught several of the tiny flakes herself. She captured a few seconds of the adorable scene using the video setting on her phone before going inside.

Hannah poked her head out the door. "Mrs. McAllister is making popcorn. Who wants some?"

As expected, Billy ran in, and the pets followed.

"Did I just hear something about snow?" Alice asked, emerging from the kitchen with a king-size bowl of popcorn. The women hurried to the window in the living room area and saw that an inch of new snow covered the ground already. It was coming down hard and fast, nearly a whiteout. Billy jumped for joy all around the living room, though the others did not share his enthusiasm.

"Hey, the blue phone is blinking," Billy said, walking toward the women who were still staring out the window. He carried the cell phone as if it was a delicate and valuable treasure.

A call? How could she have missed it? Was it due to the incoming storm, or was the phone's sound set on low? Either way, her feelings were mixed. Angry with herself, though excited, Alice grabbed the phone and stared at the blinking screen. A message! Someone had left a voicemail. She prayed it was Clint and went to the privacy of the bedroom to listen.

"Hi, Mrs. McAllister. This is Gill. I hope you have a way to reach Clint. He needs to know that I found his phone shortly after leaving Rolling Hills. I'll keep it for him until he gets back."

When Alice returned to the living area, Hannah and Ivy looked up, appearing anxious for some news. "I'm not sure how I feel about this message. The caller was a little vague, but we now know that Clint does not have his phone. It's back in Colorado where we board our horses. That does explain why he hasn't called or left any messages. But that also means he couldn't call anyone if he needed help."

"What do you want to do, Alice? We could go back to Casper and check hospitals or maybe the highway patrol or—"

"No. I'll give him one more day. I'm sure Clint is carrying out his plan for his sons, though I have a feeling he wasn't entirely honest with me regarding those plans."

Hearing Gill's message didn't make her feel any better, but she had to admit she didn't feel any worse. She could live with giving Clint another day to complete whatever he was doing. After that, who knows? She lacked a plan of her own and sat staring at the fire's flames for a while, thinking. Occasionally, she'd glance up to see what the others were doing.

Hannah had a good fire burning in the large wood stove. Billy opened up the newly purchased game of checkers and seemed to be playing the game with Oatie. Alice smiled, not sure who was winning. She looked toward the kitchen and saw Ivy putting away the last few packages of food.

Alice had sat long enough. She stood up, ready to take some action, and asked, "Should I make another bowl of popcorn?" Everyone nodded or shouted out a definite *yes*, so she headed toward the kitchen but soon stopped and turned.

"What's wrong, Alice?" Hannah asked.

Hannah's question caught Ivy's attention. She joined the group in the living room, where she, too, noticed the odd expression on Alice's face. "What's going on in here?"

Alice's serious look began to change. "I was just wondering… who'd like a little wine with their popcorn?"

Ivy and Hannah looked at each other, then laughing, raised their hands, and went to help. While Alice shook the covered pot filled with oil and corn over the gas burner on the stovetop, Ivy poured the wine for the women and some juice for Billy.

"I'll go plug in our CD player and put on some holiday music. Any special requests?" Hannah asked.

"Can you play the kids' CD? You know, the one with Rudolph and Up on the Housetop?" Ivy requested.

"Sure can. I believe Frosty the Snowman is first on the playlist."

They all gathered in the main room by the woodstove, singing songs, sipping wine, slurping juice, and crunching popcorn. It was a great way to end their busy day.

Suddenly, amid their merriment, the wind howled so ferociously it forced snowflakes through several cracks in the old wooden walls and at the edge of a few windows. The women sat very still, likely hoping this old house could withstand such violent weather. The ear-splitting sound of the wind smothered the crackling from the wood stove, their voices, and even the music. The power blinked on and off three or four times, then remained off.

Billy, now on Ivy's lap along with Shadow, shouted, "Is the roof going to blow away?"

She held him close, patted his head, and shouted back. "I'm pretty sure that won't happen. I think we should count our blessings. We have this wonderful wood stove to keep us warm. And look, Alice is lighting some pretty holiday candles so we can see better in the dark."

"And everybody has a cuddly pet on their lap." Billy

was correct. Little Charlie, still whimpering, had snuggled up on Hannah's lap, and Oatie had moved closer to Alice and placed his head on her lap while keeping his eyes alert.

"A power outage is no big deal. It happens, especially in remote areas like this. The lights will blink back on any minute now," Alice assured the gals, doing her best to put on a happy face and keep her worries hidden. She knew what problems such an outage could bring: hours of darkness and colder indoor temperatures, to name a few, as well as a useless water pump. In other words, there'd be no water to drink and, worst of all, no water to flush.

Even if the power returned relatively soon, Alice could do nothing to diminish the unspoken worry that hung heavily throughout the cabin. Worry they all felt for their men. Troy and Trace were likely out there experiencing the storm first hand. Clint, though still missing in action, was hopefully somewhere indoors. However, there was one thing she could do. Picking up one of the candles, she moved cautiously from bedroom to bedroom gathering blankets.

"Here you go ladies, a bit of added warmth."

"Thank you, Alice." Hannah tucked one of the blankets snuggly around herself and Little Charlie.

The wool blanket handed to Ivy quickly became a game of tug-o-war between the pup and Billy. "Shadow started it," insisted the boy, likely wanting to cover his base just in case anyone disapproved. He was smarter than the average five-year-old.

Although the gusty wind had mellowed some, the power remained off. Alice, being the eldest member of the group and responsible for everyone's presence here at the cabin, added her guests' happiness and safety to her list of concerns.

"Let's tell stories. Real or imagined, it doesn't matter." In doing that, the unbearable silence would be broken, and their worries put on hold for a while. Settling into their temporary, powerless situation, they all, once again, nibbled on the popcorn, and the women sipped the wine. "Who wants to start?"

"Why don't you begin, Alice? I'd like to know more about this cabin, this land."

"Well, Ivy, I don't know much, but I'm happy to share what I've been told." Alice explained that Clint had inherited the No-Name-Ranch shortly before they'd met. Initially, he had no real plans to work the ranch. "This was sheep country, not all that great for cattle. And Clint was a cattleman."

"So, he was given this land? By who?" Hannah was curious too.

"His dad, Trace and Troy's grandfather. It seemed he and several generations of McAllister men had a knack for acquiring property unsuitable for any practical purpose. By the time we were dating, seriously dating, he spoke only of the McAllister Ranch in Colorado, where he'd spent most of his life. After we were married, that became our full-time home."

"So, you've never been here?"

"No, and I don't recall Clint ever mentioned this place after that. Frankly, I'd forgotten all about it until he came up with his wild and wooly challenge. And now," she looked around, "here we are."

"If I wasn't worried about Troy, his whereabouts and safety, I'd be having a blast. Being here is quite an adventure."

Billy hopped up onto Ivy's lap again. "Why are we worried? Is something wrong?" he asked with the innocence of a young child.

Alice jumped in, hoping to change the direction of the conversation about the problems that the boy brought up again. "No, sweetie. It's just that it's so cold outside, and we'll all be happier when the men get here and can warm up by our wonderful fire."

"Want me to add more wood, Grandma?"

She cringed. No matter how cute this child was, he wasn't Troy's child, and therefore she wasn't his grandma. "Maybe in a little while. Do you have a story you'd like to tell us?"

The little boy beamed. "I do. It's about when Mommy went naked bull riding and—"

Ivy derailed the story before it began. "Let's save that one for later when Troy's here."

"Okay, I'm kind of tired anyway." Billy yawned.

Ivy took Billy to bed and tucked him in. Shadow went too. She told them a story: a short version of the Three Bears. After patting the pup and kissing Billy on his forehead, she rejoined Hannah and Alice. "He was asleep before I got to the *who's been sleeping in my bed* part."

"Good! Now you can tell us all about that naked bull ride." Alice was all ears.

"Maybe after another glass of wine."

Hannah quickly refilled Ivy's glass.

"It was a young male calf, not a full-grown bull. And I wasn't naked, though I lacked a few items of clothing. I'd left my shirt up in some mountain meadow, and I needed my jeans for a makeshift tourniquet. That's all I'm going to say. Feel free to think anything you'd like."

Hannah and Alice wanted more details, but no matter how much they encouraged Ivy to tell all, she refused and said, "Nope. Not today."

"Well, then. I suppose it's my turn." Hannah thought for a moment. "Nothing I'd call a story comes to mind, but I do have a few things to say. First of all, Trace hardly ever drinks alcohol. When he does, it's a small amount of champagne, so I'm feeling guilty about drinking so much today. I didn't think I was a drinker, but here I am enjoying the heck out of sipping my share of this second bottle of wine."

Ivy interrupted. "Troy doesn't drink at all. He pretends to drink. Who does that? He's really into being fit and healthy. I do love that about him."

"Clint gave up drinking after his accident. I don't think he's had a drop since then, though I don't know for sure. That accident was probably the reason your men aren't drinkers."

The gals agreed as they finished off that bottle of wine. They were grateful, but sad the men's reason for becoming limited or abstaining drinkers was due to an unthinkable tragedy.

TWENTY-FOUR

CLINT

The next morning, Clint's upper body creaked and groaned like an old Conestoga wagon on a rough and rugged trail. Yesterday's exertion was taking its toll. To make matters worse, the fire had gone out during the night, and now as he breathed, smoke-like puffs escaped from his mouth.

He shivered and shook. *Dammit! Build another fire.* He had matches, a fire starter, wood, and a woodstove. What was he waiting for? Someone to take care of him? Save him? Tell him what to do? No! Never! But he wanted his horse. The sadness he felt at Millie's loss was as paralyzing as the damaged nerves that kept him from walking.

Clint was never one to accept words of advice from anyone, not now, not even here. He was his own man and did things his way. What would his way be today? He must meet up with his sons as planned, but if he did not take swift and intelligent action now, no one would ever know about his personal challenge, his courage, and the extreme trials he'd been through. And, to boot, he'd miss the reunion as well as the Christmas celebration.

Glancing out the window, all he saw was a blanket of white. Until the sun made its appearance, he'd stay put. At this point in his journey, moving blindly through the snow would be suicide. He could handle one more night at the farmhouse if he had to. While building a new fire, his thoughts drifted to Trace. He was likely out there doing his best to survive this same storm. Maybe Troy was too. "What can I do to help them? I'm their father." Knowing his answer, he shivered from more than the cold. "Not a damn thing."

Trace

TRACE HEARD the sound of trucks and a few automobiles before he saw them. A light snow and the darkening sky hindered his vision. No doubt, he was approaching some form of civilization, and hopefully, if he'd calculated correctly, it was the town of Powder Mesa. If so, he'd have only five more miles to ride to reach the cabin, the destination where his dad would greet him with a warm fire, a bed, and some real food. He needed all of the above. The sooner, the better.

Picking up speed and heading in a northwesterly direction, the sign came into view. Powder Mesa, population 893. Knowing their arduous journey would soon be over, he gave Blackjack free rein. The horse began to canter, even galloped now and then, as they headed due south. Moving faster than he had at any other time during the journey, the wind chill factor came into play. He pulled the flaps of his winter hat down over his ears and wound the wool scarf around his neck up over his nose and mouth. His warm, moist breath on the fabric turned into crunchy ice crystals almost immediately.

In the distance, a structure came into view. *Thank God.* On closer inspection, he was a bit less thankful and somewhat shocked by its appearance. He wouldn't call it a cabin – a shack, a hole in the wall, maybe, but not a cabin. This could not be the location for the men's reunion. He circled, exploring the area for another building more suitable for human habitation but found nothing.

He'd followed the final portion of his dad's directions to the letter. If this was indeed the correct location, his father was up to something, but Trace had no idea what that might be. This was no place for a reunion, and why would he choose to celebrate Christmas, possibly with the whole family, in this small, rundown old shack? Or did Clint have an ulterior motive in mind when mentioning such a celebration?

Trace looked for the bright side as he stood staring at that miserable structure his dad called a cabin. "Black-jack, it's better than nothing, and we arrived first." He removed the horse's saddle, gave him the last flake of hay, then rubbed him down. Despite the cold, he'd worked up a sweat from cantering and galloping the final leg of their trip. At least there was also a three-sided shed just twenty feet from the cabin. Blackjack would be warmer and drier than he'd been in days. For that, he was thankful.

The cabin's electricity worked, but there was no heater of any kind. Trace concluded this was a summer cabin if it was used at all. With cut wood from the pile stacked against the wall, he built a fire in the rustic fire-place, the only available heat source. Even though much of its warmth would travel right up the river rock chimney that was slightly better than nothing. A wood-stove would have been nice.

He pulled the dirty, old couch up close to the fire and spread his sleeping bag on top of it. He ate his last granola bar and a handful of dried apricots, wondering all the while, as he drifted off to sleep, what would tomorrow bring?

Trace squinted and blinked, not quite sure how long he'd been asleep. Was the faint light at the windows from the sun or the moon? It was hard to tell, but he hoped it was morning. A little sunshine would be good for him and Blackjack. Still groggy, he lay on the couch, stretching his cold, stiff body, hoping to relieve the intense achiness he felt from head to toe.

He heard something. What? Was he hallucinating? Dreaming? The muffled sound of a horse's hooves pounding on the frozen ground and his own horse whinnying and snorting brought him quickly to his feet.

TWENTY-FIVE

TROY

First, he pounded on the door. "Hey, anybody home?" He'd noticed the horse in the nearby shed and, feeling he'd given his brother adequate warning, barged right in only to find a gun aimed at his head. "Whoa! What's your problem, little brother? Why are you so trigger-happy this afternoon?"

Trace lowered his weapon immediately. "It's afternoon?"

"Uh, yeah, almost. The sun is high in the sky."

Shaking his head, he rubbed the sleep from his eyes. "Guess I overslept. But, if you'd said something like *Hey, Trace, it's me*, you might not have been greeted by a sleepy guy holding a loaded gun. Just saying."

"You're right. I'll try to remember that next time. I'm glad we made it, and we beat Dad."

"We did. I'm relieved to see you, but sure glad I arrived first." Trace smiled a winner's smile even though they intended to share whatever award, prize, or bribe their dad had in mind.

They high-fived, embraced, and then stepped back quickly. Except for their mom, hugging was not part of this family's western ranch culture, and it seemed they each sensed the awkwardness immediately. Looking away, Troy scanned the rustic room and shook his head. "This can't be right. Why would Dad pick this place as our destination, let alone for a reunion?"

"I agree, but this is the only game in town. I rode all around the area and found nothing else. Since we both ended up here, this has to be our assigned destination."

"Then where's Dad? Shouldn't he be here too?"

"My thoughts exactly. It seems – Troy, did you hear that?"

"Sure did," he answered in a low voice. They'd both heard the odd sound coming from the opposite side of the cabin's front door. Not a knock, more like a thump. The cabin had no peephole to look through, so each man drew his gun. Troy motioned for Trace to stand next to the window, but out of sight, while he flung open the door.

"I'll be a rat's uncle. The thumper is my horse, Gunner." The horse poked his entire head and neck into the cabin and nudged at Troy. "It seems he wants to come in. We bonded a lot on this trip, and now we're stuck like glue."

"Well, that's not going to happen. Let's walk Gunner over to the shed, and I'll introduce him to Blackjack." They carried two buckets filled with melted snow out to their horses, and Troy contributed Gunner's last flake of hay and split it between them. They'd save the oats for later. The brothers hoped the simple act of eating might ease the getting-acquainted process and avoid any sort of dust-up these two unfamiliar males might get into. Or, it could have the opposite effect. Either way, they'd know soon.

"I see you brought a lot of oats with you. I did, too, and glad I did. It's all I've got left."

"Great minds think alike. Oats provide more nourishment and take up less space." Troy elbowed his brother before adding, "Might as well get this party started."

Troy removed the packs from Gunner's back, handing the wiggling one to Trace, and headed toward the cabin. He was happy and thankful to have finished Clint's challenge in one piece and spend some time indoors for a change. He'd forgotten what it was like to be warm.

Trace held the pack away from his body. "What's in here?" His tone coated with suspicion.

"A surprise. I brought you an early Christmas present." He laughed heartily and kept walking.

"I don't like surprises."

"Just take a look. The content will speak for itself."
Oh, yes. It definitely would.

"Why don't you tell me a story about what's in this sack while I light another fire in the fireplace. I let it die out during the night, knowing the wood supply wouldn't last long." Trace formed a pile of small sticks, topped them with several larger ones in a crisscross pattern, and struck a match.

Troy glanced around the room before answering. "I will in a minute. Going to check out the other rooms in the cabin. Be right back."

"I guarantee that won't take long."

The fire crackled and popped, and when Troy returned and crouched down next to his brother, a cat and two kittens were in his lap. "I see you opened the sack."

"Nope. They got out on their own. Hey, I thought you hated cats."

"I do. That's why you've got them now."

Seeing Troy, her savior, the mother cat moved to his lap. He didn't object to the additional layer of warmth but shied away from showing any affection for her. He was unable to bring himself to stroke its fur or even look at it. His odd aversion to cats still existed. "I don't suppose you have any cat food? They're hungry."

"No, I don't even have people food. The coyotes took it all."

"That sounds like a mighty fine story."

"Yeah, well, there was no happy ending for me. What's left of your food supply?"

"I've got one can of stew." The men split the can between them, each saving a few bites for the cat. It wasn't much, but it tasted like a gourmet meal. "What about the kittens?"

"The cat's been nursing her kittens ever since I found them and will likely continue now that she's had some nourishment."

Though the heat began to spread through the room, both men kept their jackets on. Trace said it wouldn't get much warmer than it was now unless the sun came out in full force. "When I looked around, I saw no evidence that anyone has been here in quite a while. Did you notice the clothing in the miniature closet in the bedroom?"

"I must have missed that. Been too busy worrying about you and keeping warm."

"And I saw no sign of a bathroom except for that over there." He pointed to the opposite end of the living area. It contained only a sink, a counter, and a few rough boards attached to the wall acting as shelves.

"That's the kitchen. The bathroom is out back."

Troy closed his eyes and shook his head. "Okay, so back to Dad. What do you know, Trace?"

"Nothing. Absolutely nothing. My phone broke before Blackjack and I set out. I've had no communication with anyone."

"I called you several times every day and assumed a lack of cell service was the problem. I called Mom, and we spoke for a while, but the connection faded before we'd said too much. She must have talked with Hannah, though. She said your gal was worried because she hadn't heard from you. I couldn't say much 'cause I hadn't heard from you, either."

"Try calling again. Call everyone. Ivy, Mom, Hannah, and especially Dad."

"Okay, but don't get your hopes up." The cat sprung from Troy's lap when he stood. Pacing the room's perimeter, he tapped each person's cell phone number as well as their landline, one after the other. "I don't have any numbers for Hannah."

"Try the Lucky Seven's landline. That's your best bet today."

As suspected, from this old cabin's location, or maybe it was due to a weather event somewhere between here and there, none of the calls went through. "What now?"

Trace looked out the window. "We could take advantage of the sunshine. It might not be around much longer. There's a bank of dark clouds to the west."

Troy glared at his brother. "Are you suggesting we go outside?"

"Sure. We could walk around with our horses for a while. Catch up on life. You know, walk and talk. You have to admit that we don't know each other very well."

"True, and that needs to change. Okay, let's go freeze our butts off."

THEY SPOKE of the wonderful women who had become part of their lives and had stolen their hearts, and then they threw a few snowballs.

"You haven't told me your cat rescue story, and while you're at it, explain why you don't want to hold them because that makes no sense. They're sort of cute and definitely warm."

"You don't know that I killed my favorite cat when I was eight?"

"No. I remember that one of our cats went missing and, come to think of it, no one asked about it but me. I was promptly shushed."

Troy didn't want to think about that, so he switched gears and said that he'd come across the cat and her kittens yesterday when he stopped to take a break from riding. They were wet and shivering under a leafless bush next to a wedge of drifted snow. Four kittens were already dead. So he'd scooped the live felines into a sack and planned on finding a farmhouse where he could drop them off. "This is the first structure I'd come to."

"It seems to me, Troy, that though you may have killed one cat, you saved three others. I think the cat gods will forgive you."

"Hmm. That's an interesting perspective. But now it's your turn. You must have at least one skeleton in your closet."

"Only one comes to mind, but if it's in a closet, I'll never see it. And that's the way I want it to stay." Trace stalled, unwilling to share his skeleton.

Troy frowned. "I don't get it."

"Well, I do, and that is a problem sometimes."

Troy still didn't get it. Who would? Trace was speaking in some kind of code familiar to only himself.

"Claustrophobia. I've had it for as long as I can remember. Studied it thoroughly in an attempt to squash it but never succeeded. Avoiding tight, closed-in spaces is all I know to do, though sometimes even that's unavoidable."

Their walk ended when the sun disappeared. The weather turned fierce. The wind howled, and wet snow mixed with sleet flew sideways through the air, hitting them as hard as BB gun ammo. They returned the horses to the shed and, with heads down, holding onto their hats, hurried back to continue their conversation in the relative warmth of the cabin.

Curious, Troy asked for more information about his brother's phobia, but when there was no reply to his request, he shared a memory that might be relevant to both of them. "Once, when Dad demanded that you go with him and watch the branding, you ran away and hid. I don't recall our ages, though it was likely before my cat problem, so you were just a little guy. Anyway, we searched for you until the sky was black. Mom and Dad sent me to bed. Later, when I opened my window, I heard you screeching like an angry owl. They told me the next day that you were trapped, stuck somehow for hours, in a small closet at the back of the northern pasture's hay barn and couldn't get out."

After hearing the story, Trace said he vaguely remembered the incident.

"That might have been the beginning of your claustrophobia, or it could have started the day you were born. Mom said it was a traumatic birth, but you'll have to ask her about the details."

Trace nodded and added another piece of wood to the fire.

"And here we are. I'm afraid of cats, and you're afraid of a closed closet."

For the next hour, only the howling wind, purring cats, and an occasional popping spark in the fireplace could be heard. The two brothers sat quietly, anticipating a long, cold night.

"Didn't it seem like Dad was always testing us?" Trace asked, breaking the silence.

"Yes, right up until his accident. After that, he mellowed out and left us alone for almost fifteen years, but dear old Dad is back." A hint of a smile appeared on Troy's face.

"Yeah, tougher than ever, with a crazy challenge we never should've accepted."

Wondering what tomorrow would bring, they tried to make sense of their situation and their dad's motivation. "Maybe Dad started drinking again," Troy said.

"I don't know about that." Trace paused. "But I could sure use a beer right now."

Troy was surprised by his brother's comment. It was so off base for him. "We don't drink beer, remember? And we don't have any, anyway."

"What if we did? Would we drink it?"

They looked at each other, laughed, and shook their heads.

"If you can find a way to heat some water over the fire, I'll make us some hot tea."

Trace found a pot sitting on one of the shelves and warmed the water. Troy found some old jars and set a tea bag in each one, thinking how glad he was that no one could see them right now. They'd never live it down: Two adult ranchers huddled on an old sofa with three cats and hot tea.

"Imagine that. Cowboys drinking tea."

"Cheers!"

They agreed to stay put for at least twenty-four hours, hoping the senior McAllister would show up. Was this old shack and Clint's absence part of the challenge? Part of some crazy test of their resourcefulness? They could live with that, but if not, something had gone terribly wrong.

H*e should have been here by now.* Alice stomped the snow from her boots just inside the door, took a few deep breaths, and hoped her spoken words carried an upbeat tone. "I'm back."

Ivy looked up. "From where? I didn't know you'd left. We've been hanging out in the kitchen making cookies for humans and pups."

"I drove south to the main road to see if I could pick up a stronger phone signal. I did but had no luck reaching Trace or Troy or Clint. Thought it was worth a try."

Ivy squinted and tilted her head. "So… you drove *south* on our crummy dirt trail to the main road?"

Somewhat annoyed, Alice replied, "Yes, that's pretty much what I just said."

"Oh, my gosh!" Ivy could barely contain her excitement. "Then we all drove five miles *north* of that road to this cabin."

"Ivy, dear. What is your point?"

"I could be wrong, but I swear Troy's hand-written notes and rough map of his route to the cabin showed him riding due south when he reached the Powder Mesa road sign. I don't know why I didn't think of that discrepancy sooner."

"Come to think of it, when I helped Trace map out a tentative trail to follow, we had him riding northwest to Powder Mesa, then turning and riding south to find the cabin," Hannah frowned. "I did think it was odd to ride north and then double back. It didn't make sense to me, but I guess it did to Trace. He left the map as it was."

Ivy nodded in agreement. "If we're correct, Troy and Trace may never get here."

Alice did not like the sound of the new twist. "That explains why my sons aren't here yet, but it doesn't explain Clint's absence. He should have arrived here on the day he left home or, worst case, a couple of days later if he drove or hitched a ride. Although—"

"What?" the gals asked in unison.

"He wouldn't expect us to be anywhere in Wyoming, at least not yet. I'm sure we're in the right place. This is the No-Name-Ranch. I'm also sure he's up to something. That man is capable of mischievous surprises. I should have known when I discovered he'd driven off with the stable manager's truck and trailer and his horse, Millie."

"What?" Hannah held her head in her hands. "Is there any wine left?" Before she'd even looked up, Ivy had placed three glasses on the table and began to pour from a new bottle.

Alice threw back her wine like it was a shot of tequila. The gals sipped theirs.

"How could he manage to drive all the way here towing a horse trailer?" Ivy frowned and shook her head. "Wouldn't he need a special truck? One he could break and accelerate using his hands?"

"Yes, he would." Alice knew that. Why hadn't she considered this significant detail sooner? "No head wrangler has a truck like that. Clint must have hired a driver. And we still don't know where he is."

Hannah put her glass down. She looked hopeful. "But we know where to start looking. He may have followed his own incorrect directions."

The thought of taking action, sensible action, infused the women with infectious, positive energy. Billy and the pups must have felt the joyful change in mood because they danced and jumped without knowing why. In a flurry of activity, they all scurried around like Christmas elves preparing not for Christmas but for the almost all-girl search party, which would convene in a matter of minutes.

Oatie insisted on coming. "Well, if anyone can find Trace, it will be you, Oatie," stated Alice. He jumped into the Suburban ahead of the others. Little Charlie and Shadow would stay safely behind.

"Billy is coming too. Can't leave him here alone." Ivy asked the boy to put on his warmest clothes, including a hat, mittens, and boots. She turned toward Alice and Hannah. "He'll be fine. He's quite a trouper. Billy's been through much tougher things than a bumpy ride over rough, rocky terrain."

Packed with blankets, water, cookies, and flashlights, they headed out. They'd drive five miles south to the highway, then five more miles south to look around for their men. Joyful, they shouted, "Ready or not, here we come Trace, Troy, and Clint. Wahoo!" All the passengers high-fived each other. Yes, even Billy and Oatie. Then, as the reality of not knowing what lies ahead sank in, a profound silence took over.

ALICE SAT in the back seat between one serious little boy and a focused, somber dog while Ivy drove, and

Hannah became the lookout. She felt a glimmer of hope for finding Trace and Troy somewhere up ahead, but Clint? No hints of anything good touched her body or soul.

Reminding herself that no news is often good news, she tried with all her might to push the horrific thoughts of doom from her mind. She prayed he wasn't hurt and suffering. Her stubborn, macho man didn't deserve any more suffering. *If he's merely up to some kind of trickery or a surprise, I'm going to kill him.* She chuckled, remembering how many times during their marriage she'd said that. That man could bring out the worst in her but also the best.

Oatie broke the silence with a loud, insistent bark. Alice patted his head, "It's okay, we'll find them." The dog jumped into the front seat, put his paws on the dashboard, and kept barking.

"Stop the car, Ivy," Hannah demanded. She cracked open the window, and the dog immediately stuck his nose out as far as the space allowed. His excitement mounted, and he became uncontrollable, scratching at the window as if digging a hole. She opened the door. Oatie jumped out and began to run. "Follow that dog!" she shouted.

"Ivy, dear, how many miles south of Powder Mesa have we driven?"

"A little over eight, I think."

That road was in worse shape than the one to the north. In spots, it seemed to be invisible, nonexistent. It didn't matter now because the dog led the way and didn't seem to need or want an actual road. He was headed somewhere in a hurry and made his own trail.

Alice put her arm around Billy to comfort him. He patted her leg and told her everything was going to be okay. The ride was rough. Oatie managed some of the rocks, bumps, and turns better than the large Suburban. If they hadn't been wearing seatbelts, they most certainly would have hit their heads on the roof.

When the dog veered off to the right and disappeared over a rise, Ivy attempted to follow him, but the tires spun on the ice-coated rocks, and the vehicle slipped backward. "I can't make it over this hill."

"Put it in 4-wheel drive," Hannah encouraged vigorously, not wanting to lose Oatie.

"It's been in 4-wheel drive ever since we crossed the paved road. We'll have to go around it."

Alice huffed. "Now we're looking for the dog too?"

"Oatie will lead us to something or someone. He doesn't just go running off without a logical reason. He's a brilliant dog. You'll see." Words spoken like a true doggie mama.

Yeah, we'll see, thought Alice.

As they rounded the hill, they didn't see Oatie, but

they did see a hint of smoke spiraling upward in the distance. If it came from a fireplace or a wood stove or even a mere campfire, someone was there. Smoke up ahead and some flat, frozen ground beneath the tires? Ivy floored it.

TWENTY-SEVEN

TROY

The men huddled close to the fireplace, still wearing their winter gear. Except for the occasional popping noise of a log as it burned, all was silent. Troy was the first to sense that something outside had changed. "Do you hear that?" he asked, jarring Trace out of his hypnotic staring contest with the fire's dancing flames.

"I do now. It's the unmistakable sound of agitated or excited horses."

They grabbed their guns and left the warmth of the cabin, ready for anything. They immediately recognized the sound of something coming straight toward them at high speed. There was no time to check on the horses.

"I think it's a wolf," Troy said, his voice low, steady. "No wonder the horses are agitated."

They didn't want to shoot a wolf, but they would if they had to. "It's still coming, and it's not slowing down." Troy took aim. The animal leaped through the air straight at Trace.

"No!" he shouted just as Troy took the shot, and the animal yelped.

Oatie crashed into Trace, and he reeled backward, falling onto the snow with Oatie on top of him. Trace grabbed his dog and yelled, "It's okay! It's okay! Don't shoot… it's my dog."

"Aw, geez. I'm so sorry, Trace. Everything happened so fast. Let's get him inside."

Trace got up, holding Oatie in his arms. Thankfully, other than some whimpering and a bit of blood dripping from the dog's neck, he seemed unaware of his injury and was extremely happy. "Troy, punch me. I must be dreaming because this is not possible. Oatie was at the Colorado ranch when I left. How could he be here?"

"I agree with that, but you ought to be punching me. I'm the one who shot your dog."

"Yeah, that's true. If it had been a wolf, however, I might be thanking you for saving my life."

Troy secretly wished Ivy was here. That would be impossible, but she'd know exactly how to help the dog. She'd proven herself to be quite the medic after the plane crash up in Montana not long ago. He'd been amazed by her knowledge and bravery.

Hearing a commotion near the cabin's front door, Troy grabbed his gun again ready to check it out. The horses' agitation might have been spurred on by something other than the dog's arrival. Maybe something had been chasing the dog, and that's why he was running so fast. Trace remained on the floor near the fire with Oatie; the dog hadn't yet noticed the cats.

"Mom! Ivy? Hannah? Billy? You're all here?"

Hannah pushed past him and hurried to Trace. "Thank God Oatie is here. I thought we'd lost him." She touched the blood-soaked area on his fur. "What's this?"

"My brother shot him."

She turned and glared at Troy.

Trace tried to explain. "Thought he was a wolf about to attack me."

"I'm really sorry. Ivy, can you fix him?"

Ivy, her eyes on Oatie, gave orders to the others. "Alice, get the first aid kit. It's in the back section of the Suburban. Hannah, find a container and a way to warm up some water over the fire. Billy, get that blanket you brought along with you."

There was so much to talk about and figure out, but now, Oatie took center stage. Helping the dog was their number one priority. Ivy kneeled next to Oatie to assess his wound better while the others huddled around waiting anxiously for the verdict. "If anyone has a pair of sharp scissors, now is the time to get them out. A razor would be good too."

Alice produced the first requested item without the slightest hesitation. No one had a razor. Hannah sat opposite Ivy on the floor and opened the first aid kit, ready and willing to become a surgical assistant if necessary.

"Hmm," murmured Ivy.

"Hmm? What does that mean?" Trace needed assurance that his dog would be all right.

She kept working, snipping the hair around the wound on the side of the dog's neck and cleaning it gently. "Good news! It's just a flesh wound. The bullet grazed him, and that caused the bleeding, but it didn't penetrate the muscle. This is just a guess, but I think because he'd been running so hard and fast, he bled more than usual for this type of wound. So, it looks worse than it is. It's clotting well now, and if I can get it covered sufficiently, he might be okay without stitches. I'll know soon."

Ivy finished up attaching several layers of square gauze directly to the wound and then wrapped a few narrow strips around his neck to help it stay in place. Everyone waited to see if Oatie would get up and walk. "I have one more thing to say. Good thing it wasn't a wolf, or I'd be patching up Trace right now." Everyone except

Troy laughed a little. He had too much guilt and regret flowing through his veins.

"Hey, some dark clouds blocked out the sun, and the target was moving fast, and we weren't expecting Oatie." Everything Troy said in his defense was true.

Troy and Trace hugged their mother while the gals tended to the dog. Before long, each cowboy was able to focus his attention on reuniting with the woman he loved. Troy lifted Billy in his arms to be part of his group of three.

The boy pointed to the floor and said, "Look. The little cats like Oatie." It did seem that way. They lay curled up against his belly with their eyes closed.

With Oatie most likely out of danger, Troy felt a celebration was in order. He splurged and turned the sensible, conservative fire into a heat-throwing blazer. Trace and Hannah gathered any items still in the Suburban and brought them inside.

"I'm just happy you both survived Clint's Wyoming challenge. I tried to talk him out of it, but you know your dad," Alice said. Her sons nodded.

"I had no idea all of you were coming up here too." Trace frowned and stroked Hannah's cheek with his fingertips. "Seeing you here is the best surprise I've ever had. This cabin is a surprise too. One I could do without. It's no place for a McAllister men's reunion, let alone a whole family gathering. What was he thinking?"

"He's had moments of forgetfulness and confusion lately, and this isn't where any of us were expected to be. Your father made a slight, though critical, error when giving you your instructions. You were to go five miles north of Powder Mesa."

Troy breathed a sigh of relief at the good news. "So where is our dear old dad? Stringing popcorn for the Christmas tree?"

"I wish that were the case, but it's not. Boys, we have a problem." Alice took a deep breath. "Your father has yet to arrive. To the best of my knowledge, no one has seen or heard from him since he left Golden back on December 10th."

Unable to breathe, looks of shock passed between Trace and Troy.

TWENTY-EIGHT

ALICE

All eyes were on Alice as she began to explain what she knew of Clint's disappearance, though it wasn't much. "Instead of boarding the plane as planned, he left his van at Golden Creek Stables and managed to get someone, we think, to drive him and his horse up to the No-Name-Ranch. But he never—"

Her sudden mid-sentence stop was followed by a frantic digging through her large tote bag, which added another layer of tension throughout the room. Even the dog knew something was out of step; Oatie whined softly.

"The envelope!" She remembered the fancy envelope Clint had given her just before he left. Holding it up, not wanting to get her hopes up too high, she said, "I wasn't supposed to open this until Christmas Eve. It's probably just a sweet card or a note about a future gift. But maybe—"

After a deep breath and a moment's hesitation, she ripped it open. It was not a card or a gift. It was a letter. She recognized her husband's handwriting and began to read it aloud.

"Dear Alice,

If you are reading this note according to my instructions, it is December 24ᵗʰ· You and our sons are getting ready to celebrate Christmas. You've likely noticed that I am several days late. I failed to meet my own version of the challenge and did not complete my journey on horseback to the No-Name-Ranch. I will miss all of you, and though this is good-bye, please don't be sad. I've had a wonderful life, and I welcome the opportunity to be free from my broken body."

Her eyes blurred with a waterfall of tears, and her voice choked with grief. Alice handed the letter to Trace and slumped down on the old sofa, unable to go on. There was more, so he continued reading.

"It was my choice to travel to the cabin on horseback, just like my sons. I did modify my trip so that it would be shorter and closer to help if needed –

see, I'm not entirely crazy – But obviously, something went awry on my way to Powder Mesa.

Merry Christmas to you all, 'til we meet again.

Your loving husband, father, and almost a grandfather,

Clint"

No one spoke, trying to absorb the shocking news. Her sons sat, one on each side of her, Troy with his arm around her shoulders, and Trace holding her hand. What could anyone say at a time like this? The adults were at a loss for words.

"Does that mean Grandpa Clint will miss Christmas?" Billy looked sweetly up at Ivy, not quite grasping the contents of the letter.

She picked him up, likely to comfort herself and think about how she'd answer the child's question. "Yes, he'll miss Christmas… and a whole lot more."

"But just 'til we meet again, right?"

Troy nodded. "That's right, Billy. We'll talk more about it later, okay?

"Okay."

"I can't believe he'd let himself be taken down by the weather." Alice sniffed and let the tears fall.

"I can. There were times I doubted the likelihood of my own success," Trace admitted. "But how he thought he could maneuver the terrain and survive the hardships, even for only a few days, is what I can't wrap my head around."

Alice stood and took three slow, deep breaths. "Boys, once your dad thought up this challenge, he became a new man. No, that's not right. He reverted to his pre-accident days, his macho, stubborn, I-can-do-anything days."

At first, Alice had been happy to see Clint so energized following years of depression, but ever since her brief conversation with Gill, she worried. "If I'd had any idea that he planned to take on this challenge himself, a challenge that was too dangerous even for you and Troy, I'd have found a way to stop him."

The look on Alice's face when her eyes connected with Ivy's must have been the green light that emboldened the young woman to speak her mind. "We can't just accept that he's gone because of a letter he wrote days ago before he'd begun his journey. Any number of things could've delayed his arrival. And it's not December 24th yet."

Though Troy's eyes were troubled, he gave Ivy a hint of a smile. "That's my girl."

One by one, each person's face expressed faint glimmers of hope, and their thoughts tumbled out.

"Maybe he's just delayed and can't call to tell us that.

We all know our cell phones don't work well way out here." Trace's voice carried a confident tone.

"Yes, we know that from personal experience." Alice wondered if she ought to tell her sons that Clint had left his phone in Gill's truck.

Hannah joined in. "Let's figure out what we do know. I'll start. He doesn't have a phone, and he's nowhere near one, or he'd have called."

So much for wondering. The thoughts kept coming. Hopefully, they'd generate a few significant facts or clues to Clint's whereabouts. "What else?" Hannah prompted.

"He's probably with his horse," Alice said.

"There is a lot of snow almost everywhere," Trace said.

"He's not traveled between here and Powder Mesa, or I would have seen him or evidence that he'd come that way," Troy added.

"The same goes for us on our drive south to this cabin, and after seeing Oatie in action, I think he might have known if Clint had been anywhere nearby in recent days," Ivy said, then frowned. "But we don't know the location of his starting point, and there's a lot of land in Wyoming."

The hopeful glimmers faded.

Alice sat back down, excited, and searching for the right words. "I might know. Gill left a phone message a couple of days ago, and if I'm not mistaken, he said something about finding Clint's phone in his truck after he left Rolling… Rolling Meadows? Rolling—"

"Hills? Rolling Hills? There's a small town east of Casper with that name. I noticed the signs for it when we were shopping." With Hannah's piece of the puzzle out in the open, hope was back.

They all agreed that he could be anywhere between Rolling Hills and Powder Mesa or this little cabin… unless he got lost during one of the storms.

Troy stated what everyone was thinking. "Time for a search party?"

Trace nodded. "If he's following any of the rules of his own game, he won't be on a road. Which means we need to go out on horseback."

"No! Absolutely not. You and your horses have been through enough. I can't lose my sons too." Alice was on the verge of hysterics as a new fear crept in.

"We're okay, Mom. Really. Mostly just cold, but the horses are hungry, and they recently shared the last flake of hay. Only a few handfuls of oats are left. That's a problem I don't know how to solve. They'll need more than that."

"Wait! When I was snooping," Ivy gave Troy a sideways glance knowing how he'd caught her snooping around his ranch when they'd first met. That word had history, unpleasant history. "I meant when I was *looking* around, I found bales of hay, bags of oats, and cut firewood under a tarp out behind the big cabin at the No-Name-Ranch.

"Clint must have ordered all that – on a day he remembered the cabin was to the north – so it would be waiting for the horses when they arrived. If one of you strong men will come with me, and if we drive fast, we can load up food for the horses, Oatie, and the cats, more wood for the fire, and be back in forty minutes."

Troy and Ivy rushed toward the door to begin the quick trip. They knew that if Clint was still out there alive, time was of the essence.

Alice shouted, "There's a shopping bag, a wool scarf, and a bottle of Amaretto on the kitchen counter. Bring them all and return with an extra vehicle. Got your car keys?"

"I've got the Suburban's keys," said Ivy, pulling them from her pocket and handing them to Troy. Hannah tossed her Jeep keys to Ivy. "We'll be right back, Billy. Keep an eye on those cats."

W hile waiting for Troy and Ivy to return, Trace kept busy saddling the horses, repacking their saddlebags, and stoking the fire. Alice walked circles around the couch, pausing to peek out the window each time around, and Hannah gathered up any edible items; there wasn't much.

Billy kept his eyes on the cats, but his hands rubbed Oatie's ears, and his sweet voice promised the dog he would be "as good as new" because his mommy could make people and animals "all better."

"They're back," said Alice, dashing out to retrieve the items she'd requested.

A second round of activity began though this one with greater speed and intensity. Few words were spoken. Troy tended to the hungry horses while Ivy carried in armfuls of blankets and a few more duffle bags. Trace reorganized some of the new supplies that had just arrived and added them to their packs.

At the same time, he watched his mother as she wound Clint's wool scarf around Oatie's neck, covering his wound. He recognized her strategy of avoidance, one that forestalled the reality that surrounded them all. She hugged the dog and said, "Doesn't he look adorable wearing Clint's favorite red and green winter scarf?" Freeing himself from her grasp, Oatie managed to unwind the scarf in no time and took great pleasure in giving it a shake while clenching it between his teeth. He didn't act like a dog that had just been shot.

The brief distraction from worry dissolved when Troy burst through the door, stomping his boots, and said just one word. "Snow!" The large snowflakes floating to the ground in the dim light of the cloudy afternoon were impossible to miss.

All three women stood stoically and stared at the two men. "You're still going, aren't you?" Alice asked, confirming what she already knew.

"We have no choice, Mom. Dad would do the same if the situation was reversed."

She nodded because Trace was right. "Promise me you won't take any unnecessary chances. Just find your dad and hurry back."

Oatie began his seal act – not as in Navy, but as in Sea World – looking first at Trace then back at Hannah, repeating the motion over and over. Thank goodness for dogs. They had a knack for lightening the darkest of moments. Hannah stepped closer to Trace and clung to his waist.

"Oatie's going with you, huh?" Her man, the love of her life, nodded, and the dog barked with enthusiasm. She had her answer but turned to Ivy anyway. "What's your medical opinion regarding Oatie being part of this search team?"

Even though he'd earned his veterinarian's credentials years ago, Trace waited anxiously for her reply, unsure of what he hoped it would be. "Alice, do you mind if I cut up that scarf?" Ivy asked, surprising everyone.

"I don't know. It's Clint's favorite."

All eyes glared at Alice.

"Oh, I guess not. Go ahead."

"Good." Ivy used the scissors to create a less bulky strip of the warm wool fabric, then wrapped it and tied it securely around the dog's neck. The injury would be somewhat shielded from further scrapes, and it would also add some warmth. "There. You look like a Christmas dog, now."

Tears formed in Alice's eyes, and her shoulders slumped. She handed Trace the remaining scraps of his dad's wool scarf and said it was for good luck. She delegated the bag full of fireworks that she'd planned to use on Christmas Eve to Troy. "Set them off when you find him."

"Sure, Mom. We'll do that," he said. Sadly, the colorful light would be too far away for anyone to see.

Hannah whispered into Trace's ear during their goodbye embrace. "I want to come with you. I could help with Clint and also watch out for Oatie."

"Sorry, darlin', I'm afraid not. Only got two horses. But don't worry about Oatie. I'll watch out for him." Their embrace ended with a short, though deliciously passionate kiss.

FLYING DOGS, MONOLOGUES, & THE DETECTIVES

THIRTY
CLINT

Pain. Burning, stabbing pain. The relief he'd felt from his weekly massages and daily use of marijuana back home had worn off. Somewhere along the way, his supplemental pain medication and a small, emergency supply of weed had disappeared. *Damn poachers.*

To add to his misery, he was certain pressure sores had formed from sitting on the saddle for too many hours and knew that could lead to infection. There was so much more than the weather to worry about.

He'd hated his paraplegic condition from the start and refused to believe the prognosis for a long time. He'd despised being told by doctors what he could or could not do. They did not know what kind of man he was, how strong and determined he was. Their demands never sat well with him. Then, he'd traveled down the long road of rehab where he felt good enough to realize just how bad things were. He loathed the role of patient and tried like hell to avoid playing it. *Cowboy, heal yourself*, he thought. If only he could.

A bright, blinding light hit his face and jolted him from the darkness. The sun! A break in the storm. It was now or never. Though uncertain of his exact location, his cowboy intuition suggested he continue in a westerly direction. If he left soon, there was still a chance he could arrive at the old No-Name-Ranch before his boys. With renewed hope, his plan might work after all. With the warm clothes on his back and what remained in his duffle bag – two water bottles, one pop-top can of stew, and his blankets – he pulled himself up onto the mustang, fastened his seatbelt, and drove as fast as the machine would go.

He hadn't gone far when he saw a patch of snowless ground, the first sign of dirt since beginning his challenge. Its existence was an illogical mystery. Could this be the work of the intense, overhead sun or an underground hot spring? Whatever the cause, this patch of ground appeared to be as soft as mud, unlike the surrounding, frozen earth that was as hard as cement.

Curious, he slowed down and rode closer to get a better look. The all-terrain mustang spun, sputtered, and stopped. Clint shouted a string of cuss words as he maneuvered the stuck machine back and forth, over and over. Little by little, he inched ahead. "I got this. Yeah, I got this," he muttered to himself and was on his way again.

"The sun feels good, doesn't it, Millie? If the weather holds out, we'll make it, and we'll meet our part of the challenge." Looking down at his metal mustang, he sighed. "Don't that beat all? Talking to a machine as if it were my horse." He'd lost his legs, he'd lost his phone, and he'd lost his horse. Was he losing his mind too?

The sputtering was back, along with a bit of chugging. That was not good, but the silence that followed was far worse. Clint's mustang was dead. Whether it was out of fuel or just plain broken, it didn't matter. He couldn't fix either of those problems. He looked at the sky and shouted, "I'm not a perfect man, but I could use a little help down here. Please."

Clint believed in God though he couldn't recall ever having a conversation with him. He'd tried several times today without success. He accomplished nothing more than a humble monologue heard by no one. "Maybe I should just stop trying. It's probably too late for any divine intervention anyway." Except for the brief sound of two hawks screeching as they flew by high above him, the silence was deafening.

His hopeless thoughts brought on a dizzying sensation. In a way, he wished he could start over, not with this challenge, but with his life, his entire life. He should have been a better father and a more loving husband. Often, people say they have no regrets. Clint found that difficult to believe. He had more than a few of his own.

There was no way that he could pull himself to the cabin with only his arms. It could be a mere mile beyond the next rise or over twenty miles. He had no idea. Looking over his shoulder, he considered whether or not he could make it back to the farmhouse. At least he knew where that was. His choices were slim: hunker down by his broken machine out here in the open or try to drag himself by his arms for at least a mile, maybe more.

Clint had met his match – the most formidable challenge of his life – and again, prayed he wouldn't also meet his maker. He wasn't ready for that. Not today. Without a coin to flip, the decision was his to make. The farmhouse was his only hope.

After slugging along, inch-by-inch, he'd traveled no more than fifty feet when he collapsed near a snow-covered boulder, unable to move. The sun, still high in the sky, began to fade as more clouds rolled in, bringing with them another storm. Though darkness was still hours away, the temperature dropped rapidly. In a sitting position on the frozen ground, he rubbed his legs vigorously.

When his arms gave in to weakness, he lay on his side, bending and tugging his lifeless legs as close to his body as possible.

He saw no way out of this worst-case predicament. He pulled the folded up Mylar blanket from his pocket and covered himself as best he could. Hunkering down became the only option, and thinking was his only activity. His boys came to mind. They turned out mighty fine because he was the alpha male in the McAllister family, and he'd taught them everything there was to know about ranching. He'd made them who they were, and they'd needed him for that. Not once, in his entire life, did it occur to him that he might need them… until now.

What will it feel like as I freeze to death tonight in the darkness? Did my boys run into any crazy, armed strangers or killer weather too? Oh, dear God. What have I done?

Had he dozed off? Maybe. He wasn't sure, but a thin layer of snow now covered his emergency blanket. Did he see glimmers of light breaking through the clouds? Was the sun still up? He didn't trust his senses. Eventually, Clint saw his surroundings shrouded in gray and knew that time had passed.

Then he heard it, the sound of horses' hooves galloping toward him. *Dammit. Those poachers have come back to finish me off.*

THIRTY-ONE

TRACE

The two brothers headed northeast, riding side by side, Trace on Blackjack and Troy on Gunner. The weather took a turn for the better – finally, a break. No wind blew. No snow fell. There was only the sound of horses' hooves and the creaking of leather saddles.

"This beats riding alone. Still darn cold, though."

"You can say that again." Troy turned up the collar on his water-resistant, goose down parka, pulled his battery-heated beanie over his ears, and rubbed his gloved hands together. "You sure your dog is gonna be okay?"

Oatie trotted alongside the horses, still wearing the wool scarf Ivy had tied around his neck.

"He'll let me know when he's not." Trace tried to

remain hopeful while wishing this whole senseless ordeal was over.

For the most part, they walked the horses, cantering only occasionally for short periods of time. After an hour of searching and with the sun sinking toward the horizon, they agreed to split up to cover more ground. The caveats? They'd stay in sight of each other at all times, call out to Clint now and then, and zigzag in a two-man search and rescue style. They were determined to find their dad if he were anywhere in the vicinity. Trace kept his real thoughts to himself and hoped he was wrong. They needed a break from more than just the weather. A pleasant surprise would be nice, real nice.

Troy rode Gunner at a gallop toward Trace, Blackjack, and Oatie. "I hope you're bringing good news. Otherwise, you're making my heart pound for nothing."

"No, no news, but I think we need to make a plan. It'll be dark soon. Sooner than we could make it back to that funky, old cabin. Let's look for a good spot and hold up until dawn."

"We can't do that, Troy. If dad is out there without shelter, he won't survive the night. Our search and rescue efforts will be whittled down to... just a search." Trace's voice carried a tone of desperation but also determination.

Troy shook his head. "Yeah, you're right. We can't give up. We survived colder nights alone. Together, we can do this." They continued in a zigzag pattern but stayed close to each other.

Oatie dashed out in front of Blackjack, his nose to the frozen, snow-packed ground. He must have gotten his second wind or just wanted to lead the way.

"Your cattle dog is acting more like a bloodhound like he's on to something. Did you train him for search and rescue?"

Walking so far in the cold was more than he'd wanted to put the dog through after his injury. Trace watched Oatie with concern. Was he wrong to bring him? "No, but he's shown his brilliance on more than one occasion, and he's become even smarter ever since Hannah came into our lives. I swear she can communicate with dogs, horses, cows, maybe even chickens."

"I can imagine her with dogs and horses, but communicating with cows and chickens? That I'd have to see for myself."

"Hannah selected Blackjack to be the horse for this trip."

"How'd she do that?"

"I asked her to find the horse that *wanted* to go with me, and she did. I was surprised by her choice at first, though she gave full credit to the horse for the selection, but then it made sense. Blackjack is a Spanish Barb, a sturdy horse noted for its stamina. You're a breeder. Are you breeding any of these horses?"

"No, should I?"

"Yes. The line of purebred Barbs is diminishing."

"Interesting. I'll look into it if I ever get back to my Lonely Horse Ranch."

Trace kept his eyes on Oatie, though the diminishing light made that difficult. It seemed the dog had picked up speed. He barked insistently and kept on running. Trace's worry deepened. "Oatie! Stop!"

"Do you think he plans to defend us from some sort of wildlife that's up ahead?"

"I sure hope not."

"I swear your dog looks like he's flying!"

"Dammit. I don't see him at all now." The barking stopped. "Come on."

The brothers took off at a gallop to see what the hell happened to Oatie.

After a tense couple of hours, Hannah spoke up. "I think we should return to the cabin at the No-Name-Ranch where we were all supposed to meet. What if Clint shows up or some first responders try to contact us, and no one is there?"

Alice had contemplated a similar course of action before Hannah made the suggestion. "I like that idea."

Medically minded, Ivy added, "We'd have better options for taking care of him, should he need more assistance than usual."

"How would you feel about leaving your Jeep here, Hannah?" Alice asked.

"I suppose that would be okay. The men could use it if they rode back this way if I left the keys in the car."

She laughed unconvincingly. "I doubt many car thieves are out and about around here."

Anxious to get back to a slightly more civilized location, they gathered most of the items they could claim as their own and banked the fire to keep it burning low and slow. They left a few snacks behind, just in case the men passed through here later. The Suburban was warmed up, and Alice, Ivy, and Billy were ready to roll.

"Wait!" shouted Hannah, just before getting in.

"What? Now you want *me* to wait?" Alice caught herself and softened her disapproving comment with a slight smile.

"No, on second thought, I want to drive my Jeep back. You go ahead. I'll catch up in a minute. I've got some flares in my emergency road kit, and I want to leave a few here at this cabin. But, really, you should go. Go!"

Without giving the situation much thought, that's exactly what they did.

HANNAH SAID she'd be just a few minutes behind them. Already an hour had passed, and there was no sign of her or the Jeep. "Ivy, I think we should go look for her. We know she has to be somewhere between here that funky old shack."

"I was hoping you'd say that. Billy, get your coat. We're going to look for Hannah." It made no sense that she'd been so delayed. "Maybe the problem is as simple as a flat tire."

"Let's hope," said Alice putting down her snifter of Amaretto.

Alice, Ivy, and Billy were buckled up in the Suburban when the Jeep pulled in and came to a screeching halt right next to them. Hannah waved, all smiles, before picking up a box from the back seat.

"There better be something either tasty or valuable inside that box. You made us worry and think the worst," Alice said, unable to keep the annoyance out of her voice.

"I'm so sorry. Let's go inside, and I'll open the box." A playful expression lit up her face.

Ivy's face showed less enthusiasm. Alice focused on tamping down her anger, thinking something wasn't right about this scenario. Nevertheless, they went back inside the cabin for the unveiling of the box's contents.

Shadow and Little Charlie danced around. They seemed delighted to be in the presence of *the box*. Alice had to admit that the suspense was a pretty good distraction. She hadn't worried about the men for almost one whole minute. Without lifting the makeshift lid, Alice had figured out what was about to spring from the box. "The cats," she whispered.

"What was your first clue?" Hannah asked, toying with her future mother-in-law.

Alice put on her best, though fake, thinking expression. "Let me see. Hmm. The meowing. Yes, definitely that."

The canines stuck their noses over the box's edge to take a closer look. The unusual symphony of yipping and meowing delighted the listeners. Billy had a blast and joined in with his version of howling. Curious, the animals turned toward him, stared, and became silent for a moment, but only a moment. The canine-feline troubadours continued.

"Are these going to be Christmas presents?" said Billy, excited to see the kittens again. The smile left his face, and he frowned. "Oh, no. There's only three, and that isn't enough for everyone."

"Don't worry. We'll work it out." Alice smiled at the young boy and admitted to herself that he was a cute kid.

"Yeah! We can share them, huh, Grandma?"

She had no intention of divvying up the cats, then bit her tongue to keep from saying, don't call me grandma.

Ivy quickly changed the subject. "Hey, I thought the reason you hung back was to do something with flares."

"You're right, and I did, but then there they were, the cat and her kittens, looking at me with sad little eyes. I couldn't leave them there. What if no one came back?"

Though something was off with Hannah's story, Alice chose to leave it alone for now and sipped a little more of the drink she'd left on the end table.

The young women put together a large pot of chili, anticipating the return of the men. They set the burner on low so the pot wouldn't need watching and moved into the living room to keep an eye on the fire and finish decorating for the coming holiday. It was the only way to stay sane while they waited for news.

"Come on, Alice. We'll need your ideas." Together, they all pretended the festive activity kept their minds off the dangers the men, Oatie, and the horses faced. Traditional Christmas music played on the boom box, and the fire crackled in the woodstove, warming the room. Evergreen garlands added a festive, piney scent to the cabin, and strings of tiny white lights draped from the rustic ceiling's beams twinkled like stars in the heavens. Bright red, velvety bows went up on every interior door.

"It will likely be dark when our men return, but come tomorrow, we'll send them out to cut down a tree for us to decorate." Hannah's words, along with their tone, seemed optimistic, but her eyes told a different story.

Billy, the pups, and even the cats managed to lighten the mood now and then, but an undercurrent of fear and worry was ever-present. Alice, thinking about her sons risking their lives to find Clint, stared into the flames and, with a heavy heart, waited…

THIRTY-THREE

TRACE

All too quickly, the cause of the dog's disappearance became obvious. Oatie had gone over a cliff with about a twelve-foot drop. It was too steep for the horses, and it must have been too much for Oatie because he lay at the bottom, motionless.

"Damn!" Trace and Troy hurried and found a way around that cliff and down to the lower terrain. Oatie whimpered and would not stand up. "Hey, buddy, you're going to be all right." Trace ran his hand over every inch of the dog's body, checking for an injury or anything unusual.

"What do you think? How bad is it?" Troy asked, not having much experience with strong feelings for a small pet or its injuries. He found he could empathize by visualizing how he'd feel if anything happened to Gunner or Tracker, his favorite horse at the ranch.

"Without x-rays, it's hard to tell. It could be just a sprain, but he's done walking for today." Trace mounted up on Blackjack, and Troy lifted the dog to him. Oatie lay sideways on the saddle where Trace could keep him warm and safe from falling.

They rode straight ahead, following the dog's trajectory. Oatie lay still, gently sniffing the air. Trace knew they were in a bad situation. The sky was darkening quickly, his dog was injured, and there was still no sign of their dad. Almost resigned to the reality that they would not find Clint once complete darkness arrived, he said, "I guess we'd better begin to—Oatie! What is it, buddy?" The dog had lifted its head, turned it slightly to the right of their current path, and sniffed vigorously.

"Follow that nose," said Troy.

That was the first encouraging sign they'd seen all day. When the dog stopped sniffing and began to bark, they knew they were close to something. Hopefully, that something was alive and well and not merely a decomposing animal carcass. If only dogs could talk, they'd know what Oatie knew. When the dog's tail began to wag, they assumed the best, although all they saw was a dark gray sky and a flat, snow-covered stretch of land up ahead. The dog's enthusiasm kept them going.

Snow had begun to fall again, and the only light left came from the west. "Do you see something up ahead, Troy? Or am I hallucinating?"

"Ask your dog. His tail is wagging more and more, and that's saying something, seeing as how he's wagging while laying sideways on a saddle."

"Yeah. Something is up there. I think I see a small hill or maybe just a boulder."

Troy gave Tracker the cue to gallop, and they took off toward whatever *it* was. Trace followed but slower.

"It's Dad!" he shouted, his tone urgent. "Dad and Millie. Hurry."

Trace and a glorious, golden sunset arrived at the same moment. Troy was dusting off a layer of snow that covered their dad. He was alive, but he could barely speak and did not move. Clint's horse, Millie, didn't move either but continued to lie next to her owner, keeping him warm.

"Well, I'll be. That horse saved Dad's life. I wonder how long they've been lying here." Finally, the break they'd hoped for.

"We'd better get that horse moving to warm her up if it's not already too late."

"Yeah, and it will be easier to tend to Dad with the horse out of the way." Millie wore only a halter, so Trace held that and pulled while Troy pushed from behind. "Come on, Millie. Up. Up. You can do it. Up."

She didn't budge but made a snorting sound. The men needed to come up with another strategy. The horse was stiff, but she was also hungry. Troy retrieved a handful of oats from one of his saddlebags. That was just the nourishment and motivation the horse needed to rise from the ground.

Now that Millie was standing, Trace went back to Oatie. If the dog took it upon himself to jump down from the horse, his injury could get a whole lot worse. After setting him gently on the ground, Oatie held one hind leg up and hobbled over to Clint. Movement was painful for the dog, but his voice was in rare form. He whined and barked and nuzzled close to the shivering man, knowing he was family.

"We need to find shelter, Dad. It's too late to head back. Did you notice any type of structure that might be nearby? Dad? Dad! A barn, a shed, a house, anything?"

Troy kept asking the questions while Trace wrapped blankets around his non-responsive father and encouraged him to take a sip of water. Clint stared straight ahead, shivering, chilled to the bone, and likely dehydrated. Though too dark to tell, frostbite may have damaged his fingers and feet. He was in dire need of greater warmth and nourishment, if not a whole lot more.

"Horse escaped." Clint's first words made no sense.

"No, Dad. She's right here." Trace spoke with concern but also kindness. "We found her lying next to you, keeping you warm."

Troy shook his head. "This isn't going to work. We'd better build a fire and throw together a makeshift shelter." He lit up a few fireworks and fired a couple of rounds from his handgun. Alice wouldn't see or hear them, but someone might.

"House." Clint croaked out the word.

"What?"

"Farmhouse."

"Where?"

Clint pointed, though not convincingly.

"Okay. That way is south. We'll head south," said Trace. The brothers' adrenaline pumped new energy through their own cold, stiff bodies. In spite of that, they struggled in their attempt to lift Clint onto Gunner's back.

"Call Millie."

The horse was without a saddle and had issues of her own. "Dad, Millie has already done more than her share to help out. She needs a rest, not a rider." Troy was right.

"Call her," he said weakly, his eyes closing.

To make their dad feel better, they called the horse over. She came, and Clint said, "Down."

Anticipating what might happen, Trace quickly

scooted Oatie out of the way. They watched with amazement as the horse lay down on its side in the same position it was in when they'd found her with their dad.

"Slide me onto her."

They complied with his order, though awkwardly. Clint said, "Up." The horse stood, and Trace and Troy held onto their dad so he wouldn't fall in the process.

"This isn't a good idea. You can't ride without a saddle." Trace knew his dad was a macho man. Blaming the lack of a saddle would be easier for him to deal with than his current lack of ability.

"Move me to Troy's horse." They stood Millie side by side with Gunner and slid Clint over from his horse to Troy's. That worked. No heavy lifting, just a tricky transfer. Amazing. Trace mounted Blackjack, and Troy lifted Oatie up to him again. Then he mounted Gunner and sat behind his dad.

"Let's go find that farmhouse." Trace spoke with confidence, but his gut wrenched, wondering if a farmhouse really existed and if his dad could hang on until they got the help he so desperately needed. Millie followed along. She wasn't about to leave Clint's side. Would they find shelter before the sky turned black, and the moon and stars became their only hope for a glimmer of light?

S hocked but not speechless, Troy brought his horse to a halt. "Well, I'll be a rat's uncle," he said, letting one of his favorite, original phrases slip out.

"You're not an uncle yet, and we don't have an uncle anymore," Trace bantered back.

"True, but the rat does." Troy's mood had lightened because of what he saw, and he saw it first. "There it is, Dad, your farmhouse." It existed after all and was closer than they'd expected.

Trace saw it now too. "The porch is walled off on one side with a roof overhead." They finally caught a break. "Hopefully, the owners won't mind if we use it as a shed. Our horses need shelter from the wind and the cold. No matter how you look at it, our situation qualifies as an emergency."

Guiding the horses closer to the door, they found it ajar and in dire need of repair. "Looks like someone broke in here." Troy dismounted and told his dad to stay put. Concerned and with his gun in hand, he cautiously entered to check things out. They didn't need to run into squatters, druggies, or thieves.

"I did it." Clint's words surprised his sons.

They'd get the details from him later. For now, the brothers lifted their dad from the horse and took him inside. "Wow, we got lucky. This place is one hundred times more livable than that old shack where we left Mom, Ivy, and Hannah." They laid Clint down on an old sofa then scooted it closer to the woodstove. Troy built a fire, and Trace covered their dad with several blankets and heated some tea. Oatie curled up in front of the fire and went to sleep.

"Where's my horse?" Clint asked.

"She's right outside, Dad, only a few feet away and in the company of Gunner and Blackjack. I'm going out now to give them all some hay, oats, and water. I'll be right back."

"She likes carrot treats. Brush her too. Check her saddle."

Where did Dad think they were? Surely, not here. His

horse had no saddle. A brush was not among their meager supplies, and the edible rations for humans and animals were minimal. Treats were non-existent. Understandably, Clint's brain hadn't warmed up yet.

Trace suggested that Troy try calling their mom, then said to his dad, "My phone shattered before I'd pulled out of Rock Springs. I can't call anyone."

Troy took out his phone but quickly saw the dreaded, though all too familiar words, *No Service*. "I thought you were to begin your journey from Bosler."

"Yeah, me too. That's another story. Hey, Dad, you got your phone? Dad?"

"Nope. Lost it. Those guys have everything else."

"Those guys?" they asked in unison and exchanged skeptical glances. Clint became chatty, but were his words real? They bordered on nonsense, and at times were difficult to understand.

"Those damn poachers robbed me at gunpoint and took Millie."

Again, Trace and Troy shared glances, more skeptical than before.

Trace broke the silence. "But we found you with your horse, Dad."

"Yep." Clint chuckled, and chuckling was not usually in his repertoire of expressions. "Millie got away from those idiots, found me, and kept me alive."

It seemed his brain and his vocal cords had thawed. The two brothers took advantage of Clint's improving ability to speak and asked several questions. "What did these guys look like?" Trace asked, probing for a unique description.

"Scruffy and ugly."

Not helpful. That would describe a heck of a lot of folks. Troy was ready with another question. "Their horses. What did they look like?"

"You got me there."

"That's all right. Can you describe the clothes they were wearing?"

"No, but one wore a cowboy hat with an orange muffler holding it down. I'm thirsty."

Troy offered Clint the cup of tea that was warming on top of the woodstove.

"I meant a real drink, son."

"But you don't drink, Dad."

"Oh. Are you sure?"

Troy nodded, put the cup of tea to Clint's mouth, and encouraged him to take a few sips.

That was that. They moved on to another question.

"Was there anything unusual about them?" Trace asked.

"One might have been missing a finger." Clint smiled,

actually smiled. "The other might limp 'cause of a banged-up shin bone."

Shocked and furious, they could not let those guys get off scot-free after stealing from their dad and leaving him for dead on the frozen ground. They both agreed it was payback time, though common sense ruled their actions. For now, getting Dad back safely to the No-Name-Ranch had to be their number one priority.

Standing in a corner of the room, Trace spoke softly to Troy. "Do you think Dad is responsible for the missing finger and the injured shin bone?"

"I doubt it but maybe. Everything is out of whack, kind of unreal right now. Do you suppose anyone saw the fireworks or heard the gunshots?"

"It would be helpful if someone came by to check out our show of light and sound because I don't see Dad traveling to the No-Name-Ranch on horseback, do you?"

"No, only as a last resort. Wish we could talk to Mom. I wonder if she was able to rouse some local search and rescue folks. They'd have vehicles that could maneuver the terrain, snow and all."

"But how will they find us?" Trace wondered.

"Your GPS. The battery on mine is dead. You've got one, right?"

"I think that only tells us where *we* are?"

"I don't know. It might give off a signal – if it's turned on – and anyone is looking."

Trace reached deep into his jacket's inside pocket, found the device, stared at it, then pressed the power button. Together, they tended to their dad, feeding him small bites of food and sips of tea until he fell asleep. Though he'd insisted he was fine, they knew better. A viable plan for a safe return to the No-Name-Ranch remained a life and death, unsolved problem.

THIRTY-FIVE

ALICE

Night had come and gone. Only Billy and the dogs had been able to sleep. Heart-wrenching worry and the occasional "meow" kept the others awake.

The women slowly rose and gathered in the living room as the faint light of morning tiptoed in. They stood arm-in-arm gazing through the frost-coated windows. An invisible gloom hung heavy in the air. Their men had not returned.

Troy

THE CAVALRY HAD NOT SHOWN up as hoped. The three men were on their own. Troy let the horses eat the remaining grain and hay. It wasn't much, but, one way or another, they'd arrive at the No-Name-Ranch before the day was over. There, they'd have adequate food.

He tightened the cinches on the saddles just as Trace came outside. With each saddle supporting two – Troy and Clint on one and Trace and Oatie on the other – the remainder of their packs would be strapped onto Millie after completing her job of helping Clint onto the saddle.

"Dad is as ready as he'll ever be," Trace said. "Remind me to do something nice for Mom and every caregiver that ever helped Dad or anyone, for that matter. The past ten hours have opened my eyes, and I have a new, genuine respect for them and all the tasks they must perform."

With Clint in the saddle and blankets draped over his legs, they quickly closed up the farmhouse. Maybe someday they'd return to clean up and repair the porch and write the owner a note of thanks. They all could have died from exposure without the warmth this house provided.

Trace mounted Blackjack, and Troy lifted Oatie up to him one more time. As soon as Troy was on Gunner's back and had rearranged Clint's blankets a little, off they went. Their tracks in the snow from the evening before were still visible and easy to follow. They arrived at the small, rustic cabin, their starting point, in good time.

Making conversation, Troy said, "Dad, this is where Trace and I ended the challenge you gave us."

"Why?"

Trace looked over at his brother before adding, "It's a long story. We'll explain later." Troy nodded, signaling his agreement.

"Hey, Dad. Do you want to get down to stretch your —" *Geez. What was I thinking?* Troy caught his near mistake just in time and hoped his dad hadn't noticed.

"No. I want to go home."

But from here, what home did Dad have in mind?

THE SUN SHONE BRIGHTLY, giving the snow a silver, glitter-covered appearance, and the temperature shot up above freezing by the time the three horses carrying four riders ambled toward the cabin. Oatie barked, announcing their arrival, and was immediately joined by Little Charlie's yips and Shadow's tiny howls. The women, Billy, and the two young canines came running out to greet them.

Clint sat in front of Troy on the horse's back, looking neither happy nor healthy.

"Oatie found him," Troy said. A weak smile crossed his face as he slowly, stiffly dismounted.

Ivy ran to him and threw her arms around his neck. "Promise me you'll never do anything like this again," she whispered close to his ear. "The barn is around back. It's old and, like everything else, in need of repair, but there is hay, grain, and water for the horses. I'll take Clint's horse there. You tend to your dad." They shared a quick, sweet kiss.

"Love you, babe."

"Love you more, Troy."

"Go help Ivy, Billy. I'll give you a big hug in a minute."

Trace dismounted and handed Blackjack's reins to Hannah, then turned to lift Oatie and set him down gently on the hard-packed snow. He did not move and appeared as tired as everyone else.

"Is something wrong with him? He seemed to be doing well yesterday. What happened?" she asked, never taking her eyes off the dog.

Trace placed his gloved hand under her chin, lifting it up until her eyes met his. "He's a hero. Please take the horse to the barn and hurry back. I need to hold you in my arms. I'll tell you everything after we get Dad inside."

"Oh, Clint, I thought I might never see you again, but here you are, alive!" Tears trickled down Alice's face as she hurried closer to her husband. He hadn't moved or spoken yet. Still worried, she reached up to hold his gloved hand.

"Of course, I'm alive." His speech was slow and a word or two slurred. "Why wouldn't I be?"

Shrugs all around. No one dared to answer his question – it wasn't meant to be answered – though plenty of reasons existed. Troy and Trace, wisely, kept quiet.

Working together, the two brothers managed to guide their dad down from the saddle, carry him into the cabin, and set him on the couch. Alice fussed over Clint, attempting to make him comfortable, but he didn't notice. Instead, as he looked around the room, he seemed confused and distracted, as if something was wrong with the cabin.

What was going through Dad's mind? It didn't seem to be Alice or all the pets that caused his confusion. He hadn't seen this cabin in several decades and then only briefly. Two troubling scenarios entered Troy's thoughts. Was dad losing his mind, or could they be at the wrong location again? "What's the matter, Dad?"

He tilted his head back and forth. "I never thought the property manager would do anything more than see that the power and water were turned on." He closed his eyes, and a faint groaning sound escaped his lips. "I expected there'd be a ton of work to do."

A feeling of relief washed over Troy. Dad was coming around.

Looking straight at the gals, Alice jumped in. "You thought right. That's all he did. Ivy and Hannah made this place livable. They worked miracles before I arrived, and they've been working hard ever since."

His head dropped to the side, and his eyes closed again. Had he heard Alice's words? Trace helped him lie down, and Troy found a pillow and placed it under his dad's head.

"Tell us all about the rescue," Alice said. "Where did you find him? Where did you stay last night? How was the weather? When did you—"

"Whoa, Mom. One thing at a time." Trace smiled. At last, all under one roof, the tension they'd felt had lessened some. "We found shelter in an old farmhouse that Dad had stayed in for a few nights, and there, we were able to keep him warm and hydrated. We lit the fireworks and shot our guns, hoping someone who could give Dad some medical assistance might find us."

"We've got someone now," Troy added. "Ivy! She's an EMT and paramedic. I've seen her in action. She's good."

"Thanks. I'll do what I can, but I've worked mostly with external injuries. Though I've studied about hypothermia, which I'm sure is one of Clint's problems, I lack hands-on experience in that area." Wisely, she'd brought a well-equipped first aid kit with her from the Montana ranch, and now she'd use it for the second time here in Wyoming.

She started with the basics: pulse rate, temperature, and blood pressure. After examining the fully clothed man the best she could and wrapping his hands with damp, warm towels, she shared her findings. "His skin is still white and waxy, and his fingers have areas of redness. I suggest you drive him to the hospital in Casper as soon as possible."

Clint, awake once again, didn't see the need for all the fuss, but he wasn't the one in charge right now. He requested a little conversation and a few more minutes to relax before they left, and he seemed to have something on his mind. The gals hurried to the kitchen for cups of warm cider and oatmeal cookies.

"Alice, I need to have that envelope I gave you before I left. It's obsolete now. I'll take it off your hands."

"Too late. I already opened it."

"You opened it? You were not to do that until December 24th."

Those treats from the kitchen couldn't arrive fast enough. If Mom and Dad were chewing cookies, they wouldn't be talking. Their conversation was heating up and needed to stop. No one should be arguing today.

"It's a darn good thing I did, or you'd be a frozen corpse under three feet of fresh Wyoming snow. And, since you survived your self-imposed ordeal, a question has been nagging at me for a couple of weeks." Alice hesitated a second too long.

"I'm getting tired, so you'd better ask it soon."

"Billy, go see if Ivy needs help with the cookies," Troy said. "And taste a few to make sure they're good."

"Okay!" he said, skipping toward the kitchen.

Alice let out a heavy sigh. "When I looked for Hannah's and Ivy's phone numbers, I found quite a few female names and numbers in your address book and wondered who they were and why they were there. What do you have to say about that?"

Troy called out, "Are those cookies almost ready?" Any distraction seemed adequate.

Clint didn't miss a beat. "I never called any of them." Was he grinning?

Alice's pent-up emotions spilled out, her frustration obvious. Really, who could blame her? "You'll have to do better than that," she snapped.

Clint put his chin in his hand. He appeared deep in thought, exaggerated thought. "In case things ever went south, and you decided to leave, I'd have a few friends to console me."

Alice huffed, stood, and left the room. Troy went after

her. "Mom, he's kidding. He's only making a joke. That's a good sign indicating that he's going to be all right." Seeing she was outwardly shaken, he put his arm around her shoulders. "Come on. Let's go get his real answer."

"Sorry, dear," he said. "Don't know why I spoke such foolishness. Those ladies were from the rehab center. They, too, were patients and had some form of paralysis. The therapist insisted we exchange numbers in case any of us needed to talk to someone who would understand how it feels – or doesn't feel to be paralyzed."

That cleared the air in time to partake in and enjoy the cookies and cider.

Hannah spoke up while everyone else's mouths were full. "So, here we are: seven humans, three horses, two dogs, one cat with two kittens, and one coyote pup."

Glancing at the animals within sight, Alice frowned. "Really? A coyote? Where?" All eyes turned to appraise Shadow as Alice's eyebrows rose, nearly reaching her hairline. "Oh."

Troy, keeping his distance from the felines for now, had a few questions of his own. "How did the cats get here? And what are we going to do with them?"

A mischievous look appeared on Alice's face. Apparently, cookies and satisfactory answers from Clint had turned her mood around, at least for the moment. "Hannah brought them here after taking them on an hour-long joyride in the Jeep, and Billy plans to give them out as Christmas presents."

Hannah took a deep breath, then let out a sigh. "Okay, everyone. Rest assured that none of your Christmas stockings will contain a cat and… I have a confession to make."

Alice poured a splash of Amaretto into her cup of cider, then some into Hannah's. "Cheers, my dear. Here's to your confession."

Hannah explained that she'd gone back to put flares from her Jeep into the cabin, but that was not the real reason for sending the others on ahead in the Suburban. "I was surprised when Ivy and Alice actually drove off without waiting for me, though that's what I'd secretly hoped for. I knew that was a long shot, but it worked. The most important part of my plan, however, did not."

Turning to Trace, she added, "You know how much I wanted to go with you, so I tried to follow your tracks. That went well for about 15 minutes, then the snow got deeper, I got stuck a few times, and your tracks became invisible. I had to turn back. Didn't want a search party to come looking for me."

No one spoke for a while, taking in Hannah's story. Moments later, everyone turned their attention back to the cookies and cider.

"Dad, I have a question for you." Trace broke the

silence and changed the subject. "Our trucks and trailers are scattered far away in different locations. And, as Hannah said, we do have three horses here. What's your plan for that?"

"Did I forget something?" Clint seemed confused.

Troy thought, *Oh, yeah, that and a few other key details.*

Alice did her best to ease the sudden return of tension. "Since Hannah and Ivy drove here, and I have a rental car, we have three vehicles."

"That's true, Mom, but they're not equipped to pull horse trailers, even if we had them," Trace said.

"Don't worry about it, Dad. Trace and I will figure something out." Troy gave his brother an I-haven't-the-slightest-idea-what-to-do look.

"You should get going to the hospital. Now!" Ivy seemed concerned. "And I think you should take Oatie with you too." What did she know that the others did not?

D espite his damn-lucky rescue and how close he'd danced with death, Clint still balked at the idea of going to the hospital. He couldn't stomach the thought of all those medical people buzzing around him or wearing a hospital gown. Good grief. How humiliating.

How could any man feel like a man under those circumstances? Doctors would give him orders, boss him around, and tell him what he must do. A long list of forbidden activities would follow. No. He didn't want any part of that.

They'd barely checked in and were getting Clint settled in Room 217 when he became rude and bossy, insisting that all hospital personnel, including the doctor, get out. "Go!" he ordered.

"We'll give you a little time to settle in here, Mr. McAllister." The doctor spoke with authority and motioned for Alice to join him in the hallway.

The room's door remained open. The doctor's voice was loud and articulate, so Clint and his sons heard every word spoken. "With his disability and the trauma to his body from the cold, he's lucky to be alive. I'm allowing this delay because it appeared that someone might have tended to the immediate frostbite danger to his hands. My team will return in ten minutes, whether he likes it or not, to resolve any hypothermia issues or any other medical problems that may exist."

He turned and walked away from Alice as she said with pride, "That *someone* was Ivy, my future daughter-in-law."

Back in the room, she asked her husband, "What makes you like this? Why won't you let the doctor examine you? He and the staff are doing their best to put you back together."

"I'm no Humpty-Dumpty, and they're not trying to help me. They're bossing me around and controlling me just because they can. I know these types. They have huge egos."

"Takes one to know one," Alice whispered to her sons. Clint's irrational behavior was nothing new. She'd seen it before, though she still didn't understand it. Alice was frustrated but tried asking him one more time. "What makes you so uncooperative? Don't you want to get better and feel good?"

Clint rolled onto his side, away from his wife and sons. He had nothing more to say.

"Let's go get something to eat," Troy said as he led the others to the door. "After a week of trail food, even hospital food sounds good to me."

"Do you mind if I use your Suburban for a while?" Trace asked. "There's a vet just a few blocks from here. Thought I'd take Oatie in for an x-ray."

Troy tossed him the keys.

"Shut the door." Clint tried to shout his demand, but his voice was too weak. His family must have heard his feeble order, though, because the door closed. Finally, no one would bother him.

He loathed the confinement of the hospital bed. Everything was out of sync here, and nothing felt right. Twinges of anger invaded his body, and he became defensive but unsure of the exact cause. In the quiet warmth of the room, sleep was not far off when an odd, turbulent conversation began inside his head, one he seemed part of but had no control over.

"Why are you fighting with those who want to help you?"

"They are the ones fighting, bossing, making demands of me."

"You're wrong, Clint. You're just stubborn."

"What a bunch of bull."

Was he dreaming? Was his wife whispering in his ear? Was he losing his mind? He wondered.

"Think back and remember when you were just a kid."

"Leave me alone."

"Think, Clint. Remember."

"Shut up! Just shut up!"

"Think. Remember. Remember…"

Clint placed his hands over his ears and shouted, "STOP!" This was no dream. This was a nightmare.

When the nurse hurried into his room, he was agitated and mumbling undecipherable words and phrases. She must have called for the doctor on duty. Clint opened his eyes and saw a man standing next to his bed, talking calmly, almost like a hypnotist. "Mr. McAllister? Are you in pain?"

Clint blinked. He shook his head, and his hands went back over his ears.

"I'm going to give you something," the doctor said as he administered a quick injection. "This will help you get the rest your body needs right now."

As Clint drifted into a peaceful, more cooperative

state, additional medical professionals entered the room and went to work. They were able to insert an IV, draw blood, check for frostbite, and take an x-ray of his ribs where they'd discovered a serious-looking bruise. A more powerful drug was added to the saline solution in the IV, and within seconds, a deep sleep took over.

WHEN CLINT OPENED HIS EYES, multiple memories flickered in his head, though only one of them rose to the top and demanded to be shared. He had a story that needed telling, but now he was the only occupant in the room.

Where was everybody? He pressed the red call button, and within a minute, one of the nurses arrived to check on the reason for his call.

"Could you find my wife and sons, please? I need to see them right away."

"I'll see what I can do. Hang on, they couldn't have gone far."

Troy entered the room first. Alice said she was in no hurry to watch her husband be difficult and took her time in the ladies' room. Back from the vet's office, Trace dashed in a few minutes after Troy. Clint was awake. He lifted his arm slightly and gave a feeble wave.

"Where is Alice? She needs to hear this too."

Troy and Trace looked at each other. Something was different about their dad. What had changed while Troy ate a burger in the hospital cafeteria and Trace took Oatie to the vet?

The door opened, and Troy looked up. "Hi, Mom. Dad has something he wants to tell us." They moved three chairs close to the bed. "Okay, we're all here with you, ready to listen."

"Well, I dozed off for a while, and when I woke up, I remembered something that happened when I was a kid as if it were yesterday."

The door opened again. This time the doctor walked in. "I'm surprised to see you awake, Mr. McAllister. Most folks remain sleeping a lot longer after receiving the same medication as you. How do you feel?"

"I feel a little better, and we'd like some privacy if you don't mind."

The doctor nodded. "I'll come back later."

Without a doubt, something about Dad had changed. Did he actually have a memory to share with his family.

Clint stared up at the ceiling just before his eyelids closed. Had he gone back to sleep? Had he passed out? Maybe, they should ask the doctor to come back. However, they knew by the movement of Clint's chest that he was breathing comfortably.

All three stood up to go. They'd check back later when he was fully awake.

"It happened when I was seven or maybe eight." Startled by the unexpected sound of Clint's voice, they sat back down. "My exact age wasn't important that summer day when cousin Joey and I took a walk up to the cows' biggest watering hole. The fact that I wasn't supposed to be there is the important part. We felt daring and brave until Earl showed up. He was a teenager, a neighbor, and he'd boss and bully Joey and me around every chance he got, making us do things that no kid should have to do."

"Dad's eyes are closed. Do you think he's still sleeping, Mom? Does he usually talk in his sleep?" Troy whispered his questions, and Alice merely shrugged. It was as if Clint was narrating a movie he was watching or a dream he was having.

"My dad, a badass rancher, had a few things in common with that teen. He made more than his share of demands. He also insisted that I not back down, be tough, and fight the SOB. Give him a taste of his own evil medicine, he'd say to me."

How could Clint progress from speaking slowly with confusion to sharing a distant memory, if it was a memory, with miraculous clarity? But there it was, this odd phenomenon happening right before their eyes and ears.

Troy whispered to Trace, "Dad's a lot like his own father. I wonder if he's figured that out yet?"

Clint's eyes opened long enough for Alice to offer him a sip of juice, but then they closed again, and he continued telling his story. "One afternoon, Earl intimidated us with his most outrageous demand of all time. However, if we didn't comply, that teenager had a backup threat that seemed a worse fate than the demand itself. No way would we let him have every stitch of our clothing. Arriving home naked as a jaybird would make Dad furious, and his switch would sting my bare butt, for sure. In our house, being a wimp brought out Dad's meanness, at least toward me."

Clint's words were difficult to hear, even harder to digest. Fact or fiction, those words, those pictures were in his head. Troy, Trace, and Alice wished he'd go back into a deep, restful sleep or else wake up. When would it end?

"He said Joey had to go first. I begged him not to do it and said that we should fight the damn bully even if it killed us. Before I could throw a punch at Earl, I saw my cousin with a rope in his hands. It was tied to a tree. Joey got a running start, then holding on for dear life, swung out over the edge of the cliff. I held my breath, waiting for him to swing back, but that never happened. The rope broke, and I heard his screams as he fell. The teen ran home and denied ever being there. By the time the doctor arrived, it was too late to save my cousin."

Clint's eyes opened wide, and he glared at each of his family members like never before. "And I've never let anyone boss, bully, or make demands of me ever since that day. And now, you all know why."

Silence permeated the room, except for the faint, hollow beeping from the medical monitor above the head of the bed. Clint's story stunned his family and seemed to suck the oxygen right out of the air. The fact that he could tell such an intricate, emotional story now, after all those years, still baffled his listeners.

"You never mentioned Earl or told me much about your father before. Now I understand why you weren't sadder at his funeral." Alice spoke sweetly and held his face in her hands.

"Well, dear, those were not the best of times, at least not for me. I must have forced myself to forget so that I could leave it in the past. And now, it will return to the past... and stay there. I'm not even sure why I said these things. You know I'm not much of a talker."

"That traumatic event with Earl and losing your cousin, Joey, likely formed aspects of your personality. Like the way you move through the world, relate to others, and all sorts of things like that."

"Don't go there, Alice. Not looking for any psychobabble, mumbo jumbo bullshit over a childhood memory. And I don't feel like talking about it anymore."

He'd just delivered a lengthy monologue, even though he didn't feel like talking. That made no sense and was beyond explanation. Trace shrugged, and Troy just shook his head.

"Mom, I think we should let Dad's story stay in the past, as he's requested." Troy was surprised by his father's words, too, but was adamant that this was not the time or place to continue the discussion.

Alice wasn't ready to let it go just yet. She smiled, "Your memory of the incident explains a lot."

"And I don't feel like listening, either." His comment started strong but faded to a whisper before he'd finished it.

"Yes, dear."

A second later, Clint fell into a deep, unresponsive sleep.

Alice kissed his forehead. "You're going to be just fine." Turning to her sons, she added, "Do you think that was a true story? Or a hallucination brought on by the meds in his IV?" She shrugged, not waiting for their answers. Her eyes held a blank, faraway look as she slowly left the room.

THIRTY-EIGHT

TROY

"We took his challenge. We *met* his challenge and a whole lot more. So why don't I feel better?" Troy surprised himself. He rarely shared his feelings.

"Well, let me count the ways. Our bodies have been beaten up by the weather, hunger, danger, worry, and lack of sleep, to name a few things." Trace shook his head. "I'm surprised we don't feel worse than we do."

"Since you put it that way, you're right, not to mention the fact that our women were dragged into this whole wild mess. And now I'm wondering if Ivy will have second thoughts about our engagement and being part of this family."

"That hadn't crossed my mind. I guess time will tell. Maybe we ought to be thinking about something special we can do for our wonderful women – the sooner, the better."

The door opened. "Good, you're here," said the doctor. "I've got some news about your father. Despite the paralysis in his legs, he's a strong, determined man."

Tell us something we don't know.

"Some of his medical records from Golden, Colorado were faxed to me. One thing I found interesting was that none of his current medications showed up in his blood work. Any thoughts about that?"

Trace and Troy shook their heads. They didn't know anything about Dad's medications or the lack thereof. "I'm sure Alice, his wife, might be able to answer your question."

The doctor continued. "The pressure sores presented on his hips and thighs are not typical of a man who spends time in a wheelchair."

That one they knew. Troy addressed the doctor's comment. "He hasn't been in a wheelchair for at least a week. Instead, he's survived an amazing journey that includes an excessive amount of horseback riding."

The doctor nodded and continued. "As we all know, he's spent a considerable amount of time outdoors in below-freezing temperatures. His hands miraculously survived, but two toes need to be amputated.

Trace grimaced at the doctor's words. "I suppose we should be glad his condition isn't worse."

"We can take care of all his needs right here in Casper."

The brothers stood up to thank the doctor.

"You're welcome, but we're not quite finished. Take a seat."

It was difficult to believe their dad had more medical issues than the ones already mentioned. The doctor stepped over to the room's view box and clipped up a few x-rays. "This one reveals a broken ankle, the other a cracked rib. Both injuries are fairly recent and suspicious."

The brothers looked at each other, nodded, and entered into their own conversation.

"The men that stole Clint's horse," Trace said.

"And left him to die," Troy added.

Payback time couldn't come soon enough.

The doctor frowned. "Are you suggesting that other men are responsible for the injuries your father received?"

"Pretty sure they are." Now Troy was the one frowning. "Hey, are you accusing us of harming our own dad?"

"No, but due to the nature of his injuries, I called the local authorities as is required by law. Two detectives outside the door have a few questions for you. I believe they've already questioned Mrs. McAllister."

Shocked at the doctor's insinuation, especially after all they'd been through, it was difficult for the brothers to keep their cool, but acting upon their red-hot anger would only make matters worse.

"And just so you know, your father will need to be here four or five additional nights, followed with two weeks of total bed rest. After that, I will re-evaluate his condition." The doctor stepped out, this time leaving the door wide open.

Troy stood at the end of the hospital bed, staring at their sleeping father and shaking his head. "He thinks we beat up our dad."

"Yeah. It seems that way. You ever been arrested or handcuffed, Troy?"

"No, can't say that I have."

"Me either. Let's go see what the detectives have in mind."

Halfway down the hall, they spotted Alice standing with two men in uniform. Looking up, she waved. Was that a good sign? They were about to find out.

"Trace, Troy, these detectives have a few questions for you. I've already told them all about the dangerous, crazy challenge Clint had sent you on, so there's not much more for you to tell."

"Thank you, Mrs. McAllister. Now we need to speak with each of your sons, privately."

"Oh, of course. I'll go and stay in the room with my husband."

"We'll meet you there in a few minutes, Mom." Troy turned toward the interrogators and asked, "We will be going back to our dad's room, right?"

"That depends."

Troy felt the heat rising on his face. The detectives had pushed him right to the edge of doing something he'd regret. "We each need to make a phone call before we continue this ludicrous conversation."

Trace nodded. "I've got to call the vet and check on Oatie. Who are you calling?"

"Ivy. I need to see how she's doing and let her know what's going on here. She'll share the news with Hannah." He handed his cell phone to Trace. The detectives' patience seemed to wear thin. "You call first." *Let them wait.*

The call ended quickly, and Trace relayed the vet's dreary comments to Troy. "Oatie has a torn anterior cruciate ligament beyond repair and—"

Troy frowned. "What's that? Doesn't sound good to me."

"It's not good. It's similar to a human's ACL injury, only worse. If he's ever to walk on four legs again, they need to perform a tibial plateau leveling osteotomy, or TPLO, which includes surgically attaching a metal plate onto his leg bone. So, I'll be staying here in Casper for a few more days waiting on my dad and my dog."

Troy made his call to Ivy. It did not go through. He called the only other person he could think of, Kitchi, his right-hand man back at the Lonely Horse Ranch in Montana. That call didn't go through either. "What the hell? Have aliens invaded and zapped all of our cell towers?"

Trace and Troy shared frustrated looks before each was escorted in a different direction.

TROY RETURNED to Clint's room ahead of Trace. Dad was awake, and Mom sat at his bedside, holding his hand. Looking up, she asked, "How did it go with the cops?"

"Not sure, Mom. They treated me like I'd done something wrong, very wrong, and accused me of lying when I told them about the two men who stole Millie."

Alice tilted her head. "Hmm. Do I know these men?"

It took a moment for her question to register. Son of a gun, she wasn't present when Clint had mentioned those men when they were back at the farmhouse or when they'd shared that information with the doctor. She didn't know about the two men or what they'd done to Dad, and she hadn't yet heard the details of his condition.

"Did they ask you who or what caused Dad's injuries?"

"Of course, they did. I told the officers I thought it was mostly from the terrible weather and being on his horse for such a long time."

That was not good news. Either the detectives thought she was lying or covering for her sons. No wonder they did not believe his story about two unnamed men and ended the conversation with, "Don't leave town."

Trace entered the room, plopped down onto a chair, and said, "We're screwed. They think we've made up a story about two imaginary thugs."

Clint had remained quiet, but now he entered the discussion. "Luke and Darrell were real, all right. Too real."

"Luke and Darrell?"

"Yes, I told you about those two guys."

"Okay. Good, but you never mentioned their names before."

After discovering that the detectives had not spoken with Clint, the only eyewitness to the actual theft and assault, Troy took off to find them. Trace agreed to stay in the room to update Alice on what they knew about

Clint's condition and the procedures that would take place over the next few days.

Troy returned with a satisfied look on his face and a bounce in his step. The detectives were right behind him. No bounce there.

"Have you come to speak with my husband?"

"Yes, ma'am. We need to speak with him alone."

"Of course. You are aware of Mr. McAllister's physical condition, past and present, as well as his recent encounters with hypothermia and thieves, right?"

Their heads moved slightly, which she took as a "yes."

"Good. Come on, boys," Alice said with a joyful, take-charge tone. "We have some Christmas plans to make."

"We'll be back, Dad, just as soon as we get the *all-clear*." Troy nodded at the detectives as he and the others left the room.

Clint, although groggy from the pain medication flowing into his veins, understood what was at stake. He'd do his best to set the detectives straight and convince them that his sons were innocent of any wrongdoing.

"Mr. McAllister, the doctor has given us only a few minutes to talk with you. We'll be brief. Tell us about this so-called challenge you set up for your sons."

"There's nothing brief about the intricate event I designed. Besides, I'm sure my Alice has already told you all about it. So, next question." The grogginess faded, if only temporarily. His energy returned as he faced this new challenge. He wondered how soon they'd begin playing good cop/bad cop? Clint was feeling his oats and loving it.

"Very well. How did you end up with a broken ankle?"

"Darrell, it was the one called Darrell. When I wouldn't get off my horse, he yanked me off. I fell and landed hard. A bit later, they stole my Millie but not before she kicked Darrell in the shin, his side, too, I think."

The detectives took turns asking questions about the alleged perpetrators' horses, their clothing, and the location where the crime supposedly took place.

Clint could answer a few but not all of their questions. "Where was I? Somewhere in Wyoming west of Casper and south of Highway 26."

"No one in their right mind would travel across Wyoming on horseback alone in the middle of winter."

"Is there a law against that?" Clint asked.

"No, there isn't, but it could explain why you're lying to us, making up this wild story to cover up something your headstrong, cowboy sons have done." The good cop never showed up. They both played the role of bad cop, and they were darn good at that.

"And why did your sons leave out many of these details?"

"Because they weren't there. All my boys knew was what I told them, and I wasn't exactly articulate when they first found me. Write that down on your little pad of paper. I was near death, and talking wasn't high on our list of things to do. It was all about survival right then."

The detectives nodded and headed for the door. It seemed the interrogation was over. Since when does the victim get drilled like that?

"Oh, I thought of one more thing. Luke was missing a finger. And Darrell is probably walking with a limp."

Clint didn't know which bit of information finally got through to the detectives, but suddenly their whole demeanor changed. One whispered to the other, "Could be Jack's boys over in Fremont County. Not sure why they'd be around here, but I've heard stories that they're trouble, and I think one is missing part of a finger." Clint overheard his soft-spoken words. Then, in a louder voice, the other cop said, "We've got a few things to check out, Mr. McAllister. We'll be in touch."

"By the way, they had a dead antelope on the back of one of their horses. So, I do believe the game warden might want to pay them a visit too."

The two men walked swiftly toward the door, no goodbye, no nothing.

"If you don't find and arrest these no-good scoundrels, my sons will show them some real cowboy justice."

At the door's threshold, one detective mumbled to the other, "Like father, like sons, huh?"

These detectives could use a lesson or two in manners.

THE RANSOM, THE REWARD,
& THE REVELATION

A lice located two motel rooms a block from the hospital. Her boys finally got to sleep in real beds and take hot, soapy showers. In the morning, on the way back to see Clint, Alice said, "Now that we have some good news and you're no longer prime suspects in the assault against your father, you can leave town if you want. Let's all go back to the cabin and prepare for Clint's return."

"You and Troy should go. Ivy and Hannah would love that, but I need to stay here for Oatie and to keep tabs on Dad, the doctor, and the detective's hunt for the infamous Luke and Darrell," said Trace.

"All right, if you're sure. Buy yourself a new phone as soon as possible. Ready Troy?"

Trace hugged Alice and said, "Thought there wasn't

any consistent cell service at the cabin."

"That's true, but we'll be shopping in Casper for several hours, at least, and I want to be able to call you. Our time in Wyoming will be far longer than any of us anticipated. And with all the people and pets in the cabin and the horses outside, my shopping list grows longer by the minute."

Trace

TRACE WENT BACK to his dad's room and sat by his bed for a while. If he'd owned a crystal ball or had listened to Hannah, he wouldn't be here. And his dad would be home taking short rides on Millie and grumbling about his paralysis. He'd also call his sons once a month inquiring about when they'd settle down, get married, and have children.

And Oatie? He wouldn't be in surgery having his leg bone cut in half, repositioned, and put back together with internal metal braces and screws. If only he and Troy had said no. *I guess it's true what they say about hindsight.*

He whispered to his sleeping father, "I'll be back. Going to check on Oatie."

He stopped at the reception desk near the hospital's

front door and asked if Casper had Uber service. A pretty young woman, he guessed to be thirty-something, looked up and smiled. "Casper is not what you'd call a big city, but it's not a tiny Podunk town either. Yes, there are Uber drivers around these parts. Just give them a call."

"Thanks. Do you know a place within walking distance where I could buy a phone?"

"You aren't prepared at all today, are you? You do have your wallet, right?"

Trace nodded, slightly surprised by her tone and comments. She reminded him of his mother.

"Here." She handed him the receiver from the desk phone and pressed some numbers. "When they answer, tell them where you are and where you want to go."

Yes, mom, he thought.

An Uber driver pulled up in less than ten minutes. Trace was at the Trails End Veterinary Hospital fifteen minutes later.

"Hi, Mr. McAllister. Dr. Walin has been trying to reach you, but we couldn't find a phone number that worked."

Trace thought the worst and prepared himself for the bad news. "Is there a problem?"

"Not exactly. However, there is going to be a slight delay in Oatie's surgery. I sure like that dog of yours. I'd take him home with me in a heartbeat."

"What's your name?"

"Samantha, but you can call me Sami. You want to go back and see him?"

"Of course, Sami. Lead the way."

Oatie wagged his tail when he saw Trace approaching. "How are you doing, buddy? Looks like they gave you the penthouse suite, a room with a view." It was more like an examination room with a low, soft bed, a water dish, a squeaky toy, and five-foot Plexiglas walls on two sides. Trace went in and sat on the floor next to his dog.

One of the vet techs poked his head in and said, "We had a little excitement earlier. A cat escaped from its crate, leaped over the wall, and ended up in there with your dog. You should have seen them acting like long lost friends. I've never encountered anything like that before."

"He's recently developed a fondness for cats."

"Ah, there you are." The vet entered, knelt, and gave Oatie's chin a scratch. "We do have a small problem but not with your dog; it's with my surgical partner. He's been called away, and I don't want to tackle this lengthy surgical procedure without him."

"You need another vet?"

"Yeah, and everyone in Casper is already double-booked with patients."

"I could assist. I'm a licensed vet, and all of my credentials are up to date. Honestly, though, most of my recent experience involves giving my cows and horses injections."

Dr. Walin smiled and shook his hand. "Come on. I'll show you the main surgical suite and walk you through what we're going to do."

Although Trace had not performed this particular procedure before, once in the operating room, knowledge of the surgical equipment, the basic procedures, and anesthetic protocol all came back to him. The two vets worked together with precision as if they'd been a team for years. The surgery went well, so well in fact, that the vet asked Trace to assist him with several additional operations.

"Where are you staying, Trace? Or should I call you Dr. McAllister?"

"Trace is fine. Not sure about lodging yet. I'll be traveling back and forth between here and the hospital. My dad's expected release date is three or four days away."

"Why don't you stay here?"

"Here? What do you mean?"

Dr. Walin showed Trace the small sleeping quarters that he used when he felt one of his patients might need extra attention during the night. "It's all yours if you want it. I can give you a key, so you come and go as you please."

Trace took him up on his offer. "When is the next surgery you'd like help with?"

The doctor looked at his watch. "In less than an hour."

"I'll stick around for that. Then, I'll need to deal with a few errands. Have you got a phone book I could borrow? I need to find a store that sells mobile phones and a dealer that rents trucks and horse trailers."

Trace reached into his coat pocket, hoping to find a scrap of paper to jot a few numbers on but instead found some trash. It was the small piece of paper he'd noticed on the ground when they'd loaded up to bring Clint to the hospital. No big deal, but not wanting to leave it there by the cabin, he'd shoved it into his pocket and forgot about it until just now. He crumpled the dusty paper into a ball and was about to toss it into the trashcan in the vet's office when a word on that crumpled ball caught his eye – *kidnapped.*

That word doesn't show itself very often. Curious, he took a closer look. Oh, my god! It was a ransom note. A poorly written ransom note that said: *If you want to see your friend again, bring $50,000 cash to the abandoned gas station two miles west of Powder Mesa. Leave it in the barrel behind the building. L & D*

"Sami, I need to use your phone again."

"Sure thing, Mr. McAllister."

"Hey, Troy, it's me. I'm calling from the vet's office. The weirdest thing just happened. I found a ransom note in my pocket, and you'll never guess who it's from."

Troy laughed. What kind of joke was his brother playing?

"I'm not kidding. L & D want 50K from us, or we won't see our friend ever again."

"Okay. Let me get this straight. L & D, I assume that is Luke and Darrell, have kidnapped someone, and they want us to pay them to set that someone free?"

"I know it doesn't make sense. You're with Mom, and I'm sort of with Dad. I just saw him a couple of hours ago at the hospital. Everyone is accounted for, so whose safe return would we be buying?"

They both recalled Clint's mention of the "stupid, foolish" men. Maybe they were that dumb. Perhaps they thought Clint would never make it to his destination and that we'd assume Dad was their kidnapped victim. That made sense until Troy asked, "Where did you find that note?"

"It was on the ground by the cabin the day we brought Dad to the hospital. I thought it was a piece of trash, didn't want to leave it there, so I shoved it in my pocket."

"So, they might have left the note at the cabin when we were all there. What if they go back again?"

"Only an idiot would return to the scene of a crime."

"Exactly! How long has it been since you spoke with Hannah?"

"Not today. I was on my way to purchase a phone. What about Ivy?"

"Damn. I guess we're not all accounted for after all. I'll call her right now and get back to you."

When no one answered his calls, he told himself that cell service was iffy at best. That was true, though it didn't ease his mind one bit. He checked the most recent incoming call on his phone and redialed it to connect with Trace.

"Mom and I are headed back to the cabin. My gun's locked and loaded. I got this. You take care of Dad and Oatie."

"I'll contact the detectives to see what they can do. Then, I'll go and stay with Dad. Call his room when you know something."

Trace

WAITING for news was the hardest part for Trace. Nearly two hours had passed, though it seemed much longer. Troy's call came in first. Hannah and Ivy had been out cutting down a pine tree, and now everyone was accounted for. Trace breathed a sigh of relief but remained concerned because these men, after all, had been to the No-Name-Ranch.

"Sorry it took so long. I had to drive back out to the road for this call to go through. The gals are fine but shocked about the ransom note and want you, Clint, and Oatie to hurry back."

"Stay where you are, Troy. The detectives just walked in, and I want you to hear whatever they have to say."

"Got it."

Trace set the hospital room's landline receiver on the table without hanging up. The detectives said they needed the ransom note, which Trace gladly gave them. They studied it, nodded to each other, and said, "We're holding those guys for questioning. With this note and your father's statements, we intend to charge them with attempted manslaughter and attempted kidnapping. We'll keep you informed." That was that. They turned and walked out.

"Did you hear what they said, Troy?"

"You bet I did. Now I can concentrate on taking good care of our women and fixing a few things around here. Take care of yourself, and I'll see you, Dad, and Oatie in a few days."

Trace let loose a sigh of relief, expecting only happy trails between now and Christmas.

FORTY-TWO

TRACE

Trace remained occupied, dividing his time between his dad and Oatie and volunteering at the veterinary hospital assisting Dr. Walin. The days and nights passed slowly, though. Clint slept except when doctors, nurses, or rehab personnel kept him awake and busy. The surgeon insisted he stay an extra day and night, but finally, it was time to go back to the No-Name-Ranch.

The discharge procedures dragged on. A nurse asked Trace to pull his vehicle around to the side entrance, where an orderly would help transfer Clint from the hospital wheelchair to the truck.

Trace knew that using a specially equipped van might have been easier on his dad, but he required a truck and a trailer to take Blackjack and Millie back home next week.

So, that's what he ended up with. At least he had a plan for two of the three horses. He'd found a truck with top-of-the-line shocks, so the ride today would be smooth for both his passengers.

Clint, the nurse, and the orderly were waiting for him when he pulled up. "Do you want to sit in the front seat or in the back where you can lie down?" Trace wanted Clint the make that decision.

When he didn't answer immediately, the nurse said, "The back seat will be more comfortable for—"

"The front seat will do," Clint said before she finished her recommendation.

Trace geared up for the pushback that would surely come from his dad when he carried him like a child from the wheelchair to the truck with the help of the orderly. But it never came. Clint had only a few more words to say. "Nice truck. What's in the trailer?"

"Nothing yet. Eventually, our horses, Blackjack and Millie, will be riding back there."

One more stop to pick up Oatie, and they'd be on their way to celebrate Christmas at the No-Name-Ranch with Alice, Hannah, Ivy, Troy, and Billy, as well as three horses, two dogs, three cats, and one coyote. And to think that all began with Clint's crazy idea about having a McAllister Men's Reunion.

Troy

LITTLE CHARLIE AND SHADOW BARKED, and the sound of an unfamiliar vehicle approaching drew Troy's attention. He left the kitchen and went to the door. "They're here. Let's go and help Trace. He's got his hands full."

It had been four days since they'd seen Clint, Trace, and Oatie. Trace was likely just tired, but the exact condition of Clint and Oatie was still unknown to the others. They'd returned to the cabin to continue decorating and prepare for the trio's eventual arrival.

Trace, holding Oatie in his arms and heading for the cabin's front door, said, "There is a new wheelchair in the trailer," then looking down he added, "and I see you've been busy." Troy had built a sturdy though temporary ramp over one side of the steps leading up to the porch. "It's perfect."

"I'll get it and bring Dad inside," Troy said. "It's starting to snow again. Bet we get another foot or two of the white stuff." Then, opening the passenger side's door, he told Clint, "We've got an amazing bed for you set up in the living room, so you can get your two weeks of bed rest and still not miss out on anything."

Clint just grunted. No one was surprised that he wasn't excited about the whole family keeping an eye on him in bed. Still, they hoped once he saw for himself that his bed resembled a double chaise lounge decked out in Christmas colors, he might change his grumpy tune.

Alice, Ivy, and Hannah had turned the living room into a holiday winter wonderland. A fire burned in the woodstove, Christmas songs played on the portable boom box, and the delicious aroma of gingerbread cookies tempted everyone's taste buds, even Clint's. With a little help from his sons and a lot of pampering from Alice, Clint sat comfortably on his new bed, and in seconds, Billy perched right beside him. "Hi, Grandpa. This is so cool. I wish I could sleep here. There's room for all the pets too."

"Maybe you can someday." He patted the boy's head and showed no signs of discomfort over his new title, quite the opposite, in fact.

Oatie lay on the floor between Trace and Hannah, not moving much more than his tail. The vet had said it was okay for the dog to walk on all fours, but he was not to jump up or run. At this point, the dog had no interest in either of those activities and when he did take a few steps, he did it on three legs. Oatie's recovery would take time, so would Dad's. None of the McAllisters were known for their patience. These new roads, roads to recovery, would be a challenge.

Everyone seemed relaxed, enjoying each other's company as well as the cookies, but if Clint's reason for their presence at this cabin wasn't revealed soon, tempers would fly. Clint held the answer, but why did it need to be a mystery in the first place? Troy was the first to speak. "So Dad, what was your surprise, the reward you enticed us with?"

"I vaguely recall saying something about a reward, but that was a long time ago. I'll take another cookie."

"Here you go, Dad." Troy handed Clint a cookie, and everyone watched it slowly disappear. What should have taken a minute took ten. Was he fooling around, toying with them, or did he require additional medical or psychological attention? "Enough stalling. What was the prize, the reward you were so set on giving to Trace or me?"

"Well, I guess that depends on who arrived first."

Alice spoke up. "That's a little complicated, Clint, because now it depends on which location we're talking about. It seems we had two." She still hadn't quite recovered from the dangers her husband had put his sons and himself in, and the hints of anger in her voice did not go unnoticed.

"Okay. Who arrived first, according to my mistaken

directions? Just for the record, I have no memory of telling anyone the cabin was five miles *south* of Powder Mesa."

"Well, you did, and not only that, we found *you* quite a good distance south of Powder Mesa, not north." Troy announced that Trace was the first to arrive at the wrong location. "What's the prize for that?"

Clint drummed his fingers on the side of his bed. "Don't know yet. Who arrived first at the intended location?"

"The gals were here when I arrived," Alice said, then took a sip of tea. She looked at them both.

They looked at each other. "Pretty much a tie," they chimed in at once.

"So? Where are we now? What does that mean, Dad? The girls each get a new horse?"

All heads turned toward Clint, waiting for an answer. A mischievous smile spread from ear to ear. "No, it means the No-Name-Ranch finally has a name."

Troy stood up and began to pace. "We risked our lives so you could come up with a different name for this broken down, non-operating ranch?"

"Not exactly. There's more to it than that."

Troy, Trace, and Alice were out of patience, and certain Clint had concocted his challenge just for the hell of it. Not having any helpful history with Mr. McAllister, Hannah and Ivy remained quiet though likely curious.

Ivy said, "A drum roll, please. Come on, let's hear it." She began to tap on the side table to get things started. Billy pounded on the floor with his small fists, and Hannah added to the commotion by stomping her feet. The rising negativity didn't stand a chance.

Looking directly at Clint, Ivy said, "The new name for the ranch is…?"

"The H-I Double M Ranch. Now, if you don't mind, I need to rest." Clint closed his eyes, and within seconds, his breathing was that of a man deep in sleep. How could he leave them hanging and confused?

WHILE CLINT RESTED – if he really was resting – the others moved into the kitchen and continued where they'd left off when Trace had driven up with Clint and Oatie. Annoyance with the senior McAllister man was set aside; curiosity and a flurry of activity took its place as the family prepared for the Christmas Eve dinner and celebration.

Troy insisted on cooking a tri-tip roast and some of his other specialties. The women were responsible for setting a beautiful table, preparing the drinks, and making desserts. Delicious, mouthwatering aromas mingled with the scent of fresh pine and burning logs. The lingering, nose-tickling smell of the gingerbread cookies ignited their appetites.

Barely an hour had passed when Clint called out for help. Trace and Troy flipped a coin to decide who would answer Dad's call. Alice shook her head and glared at her sons. Trace won the toss, but then a mock argument arose as they tried to determine if the winner got to help their dad or stay and help in the kitchen. They laughed, shoved each other, then both went out to see what their dad needed.

Clint insisted on taking a brief break from his doctor-ordered bed rest and asked for help transferring to the wheelchair. He actually said the word *wheelchair*. He rolled around in the living room with Billy at his side and a kitten on his lap. Oatie struggled to his feet, still not putting weight on his left hind leg, and barked. Shadow joined in and ran to the door.

"I think we've got company," Troy hollered.

Everyone dashed to the living room. Who could it be? They were all present and accounted for.

"Who knows we're here?" Hannah asked with suspicion.

Alice ran to the door before any names were mentioned. She locked it and then turned to face multiple sets of eyes staring at her. She trembled, almost hyper-ventilating. "What if it's that Luke man, or Darrell, or the detectives, or… a stranger?" Was she really afraid? She had a terrified look in her eyes. No one had ever witnessed such impressive drama from Alice before. Disapproval, impatience, even anger? Sure, but nothing like this.

"Stand aside, Alice, dear. Let one of your sons take a look."

She gave her head a negative shake and grasped the door handle. An unexpected smile formed on her face, and her eyes sparkled as she flung open the door and yelled, "Surprise!"

FORTY-THREE

TROY

A man stood in the doorway. Before another word could be spoken, Little Shadow howled and then leaped into his arms.

With looks of shock, Troy and Ivy spoke at once. "Kitchi?"

"In person." He handed the coyote pup to Ivy.

"Come in. Come in." Alice beamed. It seemed she knew something that no one else knew.

Though baffled at Kitchi's sudden appearance, Troy introduced his wise Native American friend, the right-hand man at his Montana ranch, to his mom and dad. They knew of him but had never met him face-to-face.

"You're just in time for dinner." Troy ushered the group into the kitchen while Ivy set another place at the table.

Traditional Christmas music played softly in the background as serving dishes passed from one person to the next. With generous slices of tri-tip beef, skewers of broiled tortellini, a zucchini and chickpea salad, green beans piled high on the plates, everyone was ready to dig in. That's when Kitchi offered to say the blessing. Forks went down, and the man walked around the table, smudging its perimeter with sage.

"We thank the Great Spirit for the resources that made this food possible; we thank the Earth Mother for producing it, and we thank all those who labored to bring it to us. May the Wholesomeness of the food before us bring out the Wholeness of the Spirit within us."

After the prayer and a few seconds of silence, Clint thanked Kitchi, the forks went back up, and everyone dug in. Between bites, they praised the cooks and the flavorful food on their plates.

Clint turned to Hannah. "My dear, no beef for you today? Don't want you wasting away with so much work ahead of you." He winked. Dad's intermittent charm was alive and well this afternoon.

"I follow a vegetarian diet when I can, Mr. McAllister. I'll be fine, really."

"You can call me dad if you want to."

Her face lit up. "I think I'd like that." Turning toward her future husband, Hannah added, "Now you absolutely must marry me, Trace. Or else your father will have to adopt me since I'll be calling him dad."

"Speaking of marriage, a wedding, or should I say weddings, need to come first. Now that both gals have rings, all we need are a couple of dates." Alice scanned the table and all who sat there, waiting for a comment, an answer, or a date to be mentioned.

"Fine. I know it's been a busy month, but just so you know, I am going to order monogrammed towels as soon as I return to civilization. Let me see. I'll have three letters embroidered: a T for Trace and an H for Hannah, and a large M in the middle for McAllister. The second set will have a T for Troy, an I for Ivy, and of course, the large M."

Troy and Trace exchanged glances and would have rolled their eyes had that been a manly thing to do. "Towels, Mom. Really?" Trace asked.

"When do we get to select the colors?" Troy added with a teasing tone, not expecting an answer. Mom could be a handful and took control when an opportunity arose.

Everyone laughed, asked for second helpings, and told entertaining stories or amusing anecdotes as they sat around the table.

"I'd like to know how you ended up here at the H-I Double M Ranch," Clint asked Kitchi.

"For today, I will tell you the short version of how I

came to be here. It's quite simple. I knew of Troy's upcoming journey and that the rendezvous point was five miles south of Powder Mesa. When I received no news from Troy and then could not reach him on his cell phone, I thought he must have run into trouble while pursuing the challenge."

Kitchi seemed satisfied to end his story there, but Ivy begged him to continue.

"I had a list of phone numbers, tried them all, but never spoke to anyone. Once, I was able to leave a message stating I was concerned about Troy and that I was on my way to help. I think that was your phone, Alice, but I am not sure."

"I got your message, Kitchi." That was Alice's only comment. The sparkle had returned to her green eyes.

He nodded and continued. "I hooked up a horse trailer to one of the ranch trucks, loaded up Troy's horse, Tracker, and headed to Casper. Then, I took a right and began looking for the Powder Mesa sign. I almost turned south but then realized that more tire tracks headed north. I chose to try that first, and here I am."

Troy stood up and shook Kitchi's hand. "I couldn't ask for a better friend. Thank you." Despite his under-stated gestures and words, his voice wavered with a hint of emotion.

"Glad to see you're doing well, Troy. Now, I'd like to

hear more about this complex challenge you put into motion, Mr. McAllister."

Alice frowned. "I could use a bit more information myself. Help me understand, Clint. The way I see it, our sons risked their lives on a challenge you created, and for what? The opportunity to be present when you give the ranch a new name? That's their reward?"

"Alice, dear, after the challenge had begun, and the weather turned on us, I did have second thoughts and temporary regrets." He looked directly at his sons and apologized for the danger he'd put them in. "You know the old saying, all's well that ends well. Well, I think this ended well. And that's a lot of wells."

"Dad, if that's humor, no one here is laughing."

Billy, who sat across the table from Clint, got up, walked around to his new grandpa, and patted his hand. "I liked your *wells*," he said sweetly.

Clint hugged the boy. "I liked your *likes*."

The child's innocent voice took the sting from Troy's comment. "Yes, it is wonderful to be here and spend Christmas together. But I can't yet forget that this whole thing came very close to being a total, even deadly, disaster."

Trace had a few words to say. "Dad, you put us through a lot. There had to be a simpler way to rename this old ranch."

Alice wanted some answers too. Some fast and intelligent answers so they could move forward and enjoy each other and the spirit of the holiday. "He's right, Clint, and what is this H-I Double M name about anyway?"

He chuckled as if he enjoyed everyone's confusion. "Well," he winked at Billy. "The H represents Hannah, and the I is for Ivy. You see, the ranch got more than a new name. It got new owners: Hannah and Ivy. This ranch belongs to them now." Every jaw dropped except for Clint's. He smiled from ear to ear, then whispered to the gals, "I just made up that name for your ranch, so it's not official. Name it whatever suits you."

Though silence reigned, the gals' eyes grew wide, first with shock and then excitement.

"Oh, Clint. What can they possibly do with this old, rundown Wyoming ranch?" asked Alice, her practical, sensible side on high alert. "One lives in Montana, the other in Colorado."

Undaunted by Alice's always present, common sense, Clint continued. "This reward comes with one condition. Knowing how you think, Trace, you'd call it caveat. Anyway, once a year, the new owners will organize and put on one hell of a family reunion right here."

All eyes glared at the senior member of the McAllister family.

Troy shook his head. Clint still wanted control. "A condition, Dad? Really?"

"I'll go along with whatever you want me to do right now, but once I'm strong, things are going to change. I will regain control of this family and everything else."

"Good grief, Clint. Have you learned nothing from this experience?" Alice sighed.

A look of contemplation spread across his face. "You're right. I take it back. No conditions will be attached to the reward. Does anyone mind if I call it a suggestion, a hope, or my Christmas wish?"

The gals grinning and grabbed hands. Excitement dominated their sparkling eyes. They were business partners now and had much to discuss. "We'll dish up dessert and serve it in the living room," Hannah said, already clearing the used dishes from the table.

"We'll meet you out there. Go on. Go." Ivy's voice carried a tone of business-like authority.

They returned with plates of strawberry shortcake and brownies, and their heads filled with possibilities, which they began to share with the others right away. They recalled hearing that the land was not ideal for cattle. They'd research that issue as soon as they returned home to all the conveniences they'd taken for granted before this rustic, almost off the grid, experience disrupted their comfortable lives.

"We might transform the property into a wildlife rescue," Hannah said. "Or a sanctuary or a hay farm or all of the above."

Ivy added, "The sky's the limit."

Now, it was Trace and Troy's turn to look shocked. Would they be separated from their soon-to-be wives? How much time would the women spend in Wyoming? Taking care of any ranch, no matter how small, was a full-time job. Troy spoke up, looking directly at Ivy. "Who would manage this ranch property in your absence? You can't be here all the time."

Kitchi smiled, breaking his silence. "I know people, people I could vouch for who'd love to live and work here in Wyoming. You build it, whatever *it* ends up being, and they will come. I guarantee it."

Ivy and Hannah shrugged and high-fived. That topic had been put to bed, at least for tonight. And now *bed* sounded good to everyone. Tired but joyful, some hugged, others shook hands, and Merry Christmases were spoken by all.

Alice yawned. "Troy, would you please show Kitchi to the main bedroom? That is where he will sleep tonight."

"Are you sure, Mom?"

"Yes. I want to spend some time in the kitchen, and then I want to be alone with my husband." The gals tried to object and offered to take charge of the cleanup, but Alice said they'd already done enough and insisted they get some rest.

Kitchi invited Billy to sleep in the large main bedroom with him. "There's room for Shadow too."

"Can I, Daddy? Please!"

Was his offer real? It seemed too good to be true. Troy looked at Kitchi, who promptly gave a nod. No words were needed. Troy's eyes met Ivy's, they grasped hands and headed down the hall.

Billy dashed back to his grandpa and whispered in his ear. "I heard that Kitchi-man tell my daddy that you were looking for your spirit. Did you find it?"

"Can I let you know tomorrow?"

"Yes, sir!" And off he marched to the big bedroom for a sleepover with Kitchi and the coyote.

C lint and Alice lay side by side on the oversized hospital bed that masqueraded as a chaise lounge. With their heads slightly raised, they watched the flames flicker through the woodstove's glass door.

"I'm glad you're here with me, Alice. I had a lot of time to think out there with nothing but sky, snow, and freezing temperatures. I missed you more than you'll ever know."

"Someday, I want to hear every detail of your journey but not tonight. There were days when I thought I'd never see you again or know if you were dead or alive. Right now, I just need to be close to you, feel your warmth and your beating heart." She turned on her side and put her head on his shoulder.

"Be patient with me, Alice. There are a few things I must get off my chest. I was wrong to put our sons in danger; I was wrong to keep the fact that I'd be riding horseback across Wyoming from you; it was my fault that Millie was stolen and almost lost forever; and, without a doubt, I was responsible for Rowdy's untimely, unnecessary death years ago too. I doubt I'll ever be able to forgive myself for causing so much trouble."

That was the first time Clint mentioned the death of his horse since the horrific accident occurred. He'd argued with Alice and stormed from the ranch on the horse's back, downing a bottle of Wild Turkey as he rode. He tried but couldn't remember what the argument was about. All he could recall was being crazy and foolish. "Why did we argue? Do you remember?" He had a feeling he wouldn't like her answer, but honestly, he couldn't remember.

She shook her head, unconvincingly.

"Come on, think. How many times in your life have you said, *I can forgive, but I can't forget*?"

"All right. I just said you'd had too much to drink and needed to stop, or I would leave."

He closed his eyes, embarrassed. The dark memories he'd erased came to light like a flashing neon sign. Although anger didn't come this time as it often had in the past, remorse did. Tonight, he remembered everything in living color and with a soundtrack, as if watching a movie with too much drama.

He had argued with his wife and said horrible, senseless things. All by himself, he'd emptied an entire bottle filled with Wild Turkey, and his careless gallop up the steep, rocky ridge near the lake cabin caused his horse, Rowdy, to fall and break its leg. The horse had to be put down because of him. And now, he had to take full responsibility for the loss of his legs, too, and for distancing himself from his family. "Are you going to leave me, Alice? I wouldn't blame you if you did."

"No, Clint. For better or worse, it's you and me together forever." As the hour grew late, their breathing slowed, and their eyelids fluttered, fighting to remain open a little while longer. Still holding hands, Alice whispered, "Tell me just one thing, Clint."

"Something in particular?"

"Yes. Tell me about the moment you knew you were saved, and your life would go on."

"All right. I can do that. At that point, *thinking* was the only activity I could do. Though my thoughts were not always rational, I'll never forget that moment. As I lay on the frozen ground, Millie at my side, another round of light snow had begun to fall, though the sky to the west was nearly clear. Two conflicting thoughts occupied my mind as I stared at the horizon that evening. First, that I'd been blessed to witness the most beautiful sunset there ever could be, and second, it was certain to be my last."

He brushed away the tears trickling from the corners of Alice's eyes and continued, though his voice trembled, and his words trailed out as a whisper. "Just as the final beam of golden light dipped silently behind the hills, Trace and Troy and Oatie arrived. Then, it seemed as if a peaceful veil of gray had tucked me in for the night." He'd answered her question. Would that be enough talking for now?

"Thank you, Clint. That was a miracle. I hope you know that."

He nodded. Folks often said this was the season of miracles, but he wondered if he deserved one. "Now that I am here with you, our boys, and the new members of our family, I feel renewed, almost whole again." He stroked her face, and when she gazed at him with loving eyes, he returned that look and kissed her gently.

His family's insightful actions, perseverance, and love made it possible for Clint to face tomorrow with a contented smile. Tomorrow. Yes, there would be a tomorrow. He liked the sound of that. It seemed the challenge he'd proposed and his own ride across Wyoming set into motion a more profound significance, a new kind of journey, one that had only just begun.

"I've been given a second chance, Alice. I will

forever remember that transformative moment as I lay on the ground half-frozen and certain the end was near. For my remaining days on this great earth, every sundown will remind me that tomorrow is just a blink away, and with it comes another opportunity to love and be loved. Alice, I love you and our boys—"

"They're *men*, Clint."

He smiled and patted her hand. "You just had to have the last word, huh?"

"Yes."

The cabin was silent, the sun not yet up, and the fire barely flickered in the woodstove. Clint felt a tapping, a gentle patting on his arm. His eyes struggled to open. It was little Billy, the first one up.

"Did you find your spirit, Grandpa?" the boy whispered.

Clint smiled weakly, still groggy from sleep and his nighttime pain medication. "I did find it, and I think I found the Christmas Spirit too."

"Wow!" Billy's hands went up to his cheeks. "This is the best Christmas ever, huh?"

"You might be right about that. Hey, do you want to hop up and get in bed with us?"

No verbal answer came, but all of a sudden, there they were: grandpa, grandma, and little Billy in the middle. "Santa has been here! He found us. There are so many presents under the tree. I never saw that many in my whole life."

Clint looked toward the tree. He'd never seen so many presents either. "Santa must have a lot of elves working this year, and they've all been very busy."

Troy was the next McAllister to enter the living room. He added more logs to the drowsy fire; the room would be warm before the others woke up.

"Mornin', Troy."

"Merry Christmas, Dad, Mom, Billy."

Troy told Clint the night before that he wanted Billy to have a wonderful Santa experience and that most of his purchases were gifts for the boy. However, the tags would say they were from Santa. He'd also mentioned that on one of his trips back to Casper, he'd taken Billy with him to help purchase the fixings for Christmas Eve dinner and Christmas breakfast. While they were there, they picked out a present for every pet. Yes, even the cats because Billy wasn't sure Santa would bring them anything.

"I'll be in the kitchen whipping up some breakfast," Troy said, leaving the room.

It wasn't long before the delicious aroma of bacon, eggs, potatoes O'Brien, and coffee permeated the air and could not be ignored. In a matter of minutes, Trace and the gals gathered around the bed to say good morning to

Clint, Alice, and Billy before following the irresistible smells. They all had sleepy eyes, tousled hair, and were still wearing pajamas – all except Troy and Trace. They wore jeans, western shirts, and cowboy boots. Neither men were the pajama type.

Clint noticed the looks of surprise on everyone's face when they saw all the presents under the tree. He found that phenomenon quite puzzling. Maybe Santa really *had* stopped by last night.

Kitchi was the last to arrive at the table, though now they all knew why. He'd gotten up early to check on Blackjack, Gunner, Millie, and Tracker. The kittens bounced around, chasing their tails and each other. Little Charlie and Shadow dashed around the table, stopping now and then to sniff the delicious smells that filled the air. The mother cat spent most of her time lying with Oatie near the woodstove, so Billy delivered two bowls, each containing a breakfast prepared just for them. The H-I Double M Ranch overflowed with people, animals, and an abundance of joy!

After breakfast, as they opened presents, it became apparent that everyone had found a way to accomplish a bit of secret shopping and the covert placement of their gifts under the tree sometime during the night. Everyone but Clint, that is. Although there were a few presents for Clint, none of the presents under the tree were from him.

No one spoke of this out loud, not wanting anything to upset him today. There was no way he could have shopped. "It's okay, Grandpa. Santa brought enough for everyone," Billy said, smiling. Did the child just wink?

Something set the dogs to barking, and even Shadow, the cats, and Oatie went to the front door. Billy heard bells jingling and gasped. "It must be Santa!" He ran to the window. "No Santa. Just more horses pulling a... pulling something. Look!"

The biggest surprise of all came from Clint. He couldn't take credit for the two feet of newly fallen snow, but before leaving Golden, Colorado, he'd arranged for the delivery of a horse-drawn carriage on Christmas Day. It arrived right on time at the correct location, complete with jingle bells and room for everyone. No mistakes made today, though he had to laugh at the current surplus of horses at the H-I Double M Ranch.

"Get dressed, everyone. Our carriage awaits."

End of Book 3
In The McAllister Brothers Series

Author's Note

It was time to bring the entire McAllister family together, but how would I do that? To begin with, all I had was: Clint, the senior McAllister man, challenging his sons, Trace and Troy, to ride across Wyoming in the middle of winter on horseback. Two cowboys and two horses riding in different directions does not a novel make. Dialogue would be sorely limited. Despite sibling rivalry and strong male egos, each cowboy journeyed onward in his own way.

Turning that brief concept into a novel required saddle-bags full of imagination and stacks of research materials. I had no one to blame but myself for this daunting challenge. At times I regretted my premise and wanted to give up. Finally, I took my first real step and began a sketchy outline even though I had next to nothing from my own life to draw upon, or so I thought at the time. I'd never sat on the back of a real horse, and I doubt the coin-operated, fake pony outside the grocery store counted. I never had any coins anyway.

Then I remembered my father, a serious, hardworking, stern man when it came to raising his children. Out in the world, he thought he could accomplish anything. Sometimes he did. Yes, Clint and my dad were the same in many ways. Still, it wasn't until I included the women's perspectives that **Wyoming Sundown** took off and almost wrote itself. Thanks, Ladies! Of course, the presence of horses, felines, canines, a young boy, and a wise Native American man played a role in bringing safety, delight, joy, and miracles to the McAllister family.

To this day, I hope to meet up with another coin-operated pony. I still want to mount that horse, and I will have enough coins in my pocket for a lengthy ride.

I hope you enjoyed Wyoming Sundown. Sometime next year, Books 4 & 5 featuring Alice, Hannah, and Ivy, the magnificent McAllister women, will be released. Happy Trails until then.

Cricket

WHAT? YOU MISSED BOOK 1 OR BOOK 2?

No worries. It's not too late to catch up.

COLORADO TAKEDOWN

Book 1 in The McAllister Brothers Series

A vegetarian from the city and a cattle-raising rancher sounds like a match made in hell. But what if they need each other more than they realize? How will Hannah deal with becoming a novice rancher and a fake widow all in one day?

MONTANA COUNTDOWN

Book 2 in The McAllister Brothers Series

Troy, a wealthy rancher and Ivy, a beautiful, would-be novelist team up to save the ranch from unthinkable evil and end up fighting for their lives. It seemed the end was near when an unexpected visitor shocked them all.

GUNNER'S STORY

The horse, Gunner, who appears in MONTANA COUNT-
DOWN and WYOMING SUNDOWN was inspired by a
real horse that was rescued from 400 acres of desert on
February 16, 2015 by HEART OF TUCSON.

No one knows for sure how long he'd been wandering
in this southern Arizona desert, but he was skinny, had an
injury on his back leg, and needed to be cared for.

When a nearby skeet range called the rescue threatening to shoot this horse if it wasn't removed, time was of the essence.

Upon reaching the area where the horse had been seen, his rescuers heard gunfire from two directions. One being the skeet range, the other? Unknown persons firing bullets. No rescue took place that day, but they returned the next day to try again.

With alfalfa, apples, and carrots in hand, and five hours of patience and trust building, they coaxed the lonely, hungry horse into the trailer and took him to the HEART property and named him Gunner.

You can find out more about the HEART OF TUCSON horse rescue on their website or Facebook page.

http://heartoftucson.org/

www.facebook.com/heartoftucson

BLACKJACK'S STORY

I gave the horse in WYOMING SUNDOWN, the name
Blackjack. He is the horse that Trace McAllister rides

across Wyoming in the middle of winter. Trace's horse is a Spanish Barb.

The Spanish Barb Horse Association (SBHA), formerly known as the Spanish Barb Breeders Association (SBBA) is dedicated to the preservation and promotion of the Spanish Barb Horse. They have changed their name but not their mission. The Spanish horse was made to build the West, and that it did!

You can learn more about this amazing breed at the following locations:

www.spanishbarb.com

https://www.facebook.com/groups/130122983703371/

The original Blackjack, the last of the United States Army Quartermaster issued horses, was born on January 19, 1947. He entered the Third United States Infantry Stables at Fort Myer in 1953.

During his service as a caparisoned (riderless horse), Blackjack took part in the funerals of Presidents Herbert Hoover, John F. Kennedy and Lyndon B. Johnson and that of the General of the Army, Douglas MacArthur.

When he died on February 6, 1976, Blackjack was laid to rest on the parade ground at Fort Myer, Virginia.

THANK YOU!

Thank you for reading *Wyoming Sundown*.
Would you like to know when the next book in the
McAllister Brothers series is available? That's easy. Sign
up for Cricket's (almost) monthly NEWSLETTER and
you'll receive notifications of new books, giveaways, and
other exclusive content.

If you enjoyed this story, please leave a REVIEW
on Goodreads, Bookbub, or your favorite online retailer.
Reviews are helpful to readers and appreciated by
authors.

ABOUT THE AUTHOR

Cricket Rohman grew up in Estes Park, Colorado and spent her formative years among deer, coyotes, and fields of beautiful blue columbine. After retiring from a career in education, she became a full-time author writing contemporary fiction and western series and sagas about teachers, cowboys, dogs, lovers, and creative women inventing unique careers—just to mention a few.

Cricket loves to hear from readers.
Connect with her via:

Website http://www.cricketrohman.org
Facebook https://facebook.com/CricketRohmanAuthor
Twitter https://twitter.com/CricketRohman
Bookbub https://www.bookbub.com/authors/cricket-rohman
Email cricketrohman@gmail.com

You will find the links & excerpts for all of Cricket Rohman's books at

www.cricketrohman.org

The McAllister Brothers Series

Romantic Western Adventures

COLORADO TAKEDOWN, Book 1

This twisty cowboy adventure includes treachery, new love, family, courage, and amazing ranch animals.

MONTANA COUNTDOWN, Book 2

A wealthy rancher's story-telling tendency entices two eavesdroppers—a greedy criminal and a would-be novelist—to venture to his Montana ranch to search for his hidden treasure.

WYOMING SUNDOWN, Book 3

Clint McAllister's challenge put his sons in grave danger. Alice is furious about his foolish plan. It was almost Christmas, a bad time for such nonsense.

The Creative Hearts Sweet Romance Series

Creative Women Standalone Novellas

PHOEBE'S PHOTO FETISH

Phoebe Foxglove had three loves: Photography, Flowers, and Bobby. Two out of the three served her well.

ANNA'S ANIMAL HOUSE

Anna's new life began the moment she caught a glimpse of the flashing red light. There was no turning back now. But what was up ahead?

CAITLIN'S COW WASH

Caitlin feels trapped and out of place living in an old-fashion *Leave It To Beaver* household. Then, a perfect, win-win solution comes along—a cowboy named Cooper.

TINA'S TASTY TOURS

Tina has an impossible dream that comes with a substantial price tag. In the meantime, she works at the Punk Patio and a 1960s diner where she is required to look like Marilyn Monroe.

The Lindsey Lark Series

Fiction with Elements of Romance & Mystery

WANTED: AN HONEST MAN

Lindsey, a kinder teacher in survival mode after an unthinkable divorce, is brilliant in the classroom. Unfortunately, unwanted sinister challenges invade her off-hours.

LETTERS, LOVERS, & LIES

Jake and Lindsey are in love, but so much stands in their way. Fortunately, they are smart, multi-talented, and they love to laugh. Wendell, the 180-pound mastiff, is featured throughout this series.

HIT THE ROAD, JAKE!

Thrilling, romantic, and sprinkled with humor, this novel reinvents the 'buddy movie' concept with the written word … and a pretty woman. As Jake and Lindsey travel from Tucson to Estes Park in their RV, the dangers they face become deadly.

The Fantasy Maker Series

Contemporary Adventures

FOREVER ISLAND

JD won a contest and ended up on a deserted island somewhere in Micronesia. This is a wild beach adventure complete with danger, love, and a dog named Noodles.

WINTER'S BLUSH

The Fantasy Maker strikes an agreement with Clay. What's the catch? He must pretend to be someone he's not. A quick read that includes mountain hiking, rescue dogs, danger, and yes, some romance.

Saving Madeline

Standalone Contemporary Fiction

An entertaining story with humor, emotion, and an unusual mother-daughter relationship.

Christmas in the North Woods

A Children's Picture Book

Oliver Owl introduces the reader to his forest friends who are busy rehearsing for the annual Christmas Song Contest.